*SLEEPING CHILDREN*

# SLEEPING CHILDREN

*A Novel*

## Anthony Passeron

*Translated from the French by Frank Wynne*

FARRAR, STRAUS AND GIROUX

NEW YORK

Farrar, Straus and Giroux
120 Broadway, New York 10271

Copyright © 2022 by éditions Globe
Translation copyright © 2025 by Frank Wynne
All rights reserved
Printed in the United States of America
Originally published in French in 2022 by éditions Globe, France, as *Les enfants endormis*
English translation first published in 2025 by Picador, Great Britain
English translation published in the United States by Farrar, Straus and Giroux
First American edition, 2025

Library of Congress Cataloging-in-Publication Data
Names: Passeron, Anthony, 1983– author. | Wynne, Frank, translator.
Title: Sleeping children : a novel / Anthony Passeron ; translated from the French by Frank Wynne.
Other titles: Enfants endormis. English
Description: First American edition. | New York : Farrar, Straus and Giroux, 2025. | "Originally published in French in 2022 by éditions Globe, France, as Les enfants endormis"—Title page verso.
Identifiers: LCCN 2024053302 | ISBN 9780374612269 (hardcover)
Subjects: LCGFT: Novels.
Classification: LCC PQ2716.A37726 E5413 2025 | DDC 843/.92—dc23/eng/20241202
LC record available at https://lccn.loc.gov/2024053302

Our books may be purchased in bulk for promotional, educational, or business use. Please contact your local bookseller or the Macmillan Corporate and Premium Sales Department at 1-800-221-7945, extension 5442, or by email at MacmillanSpecialMarkets@macmillan.com.

www.fsgbooks.com
Follow us on social media at @fsgbooks

1  3  5  7  9  10  8  6  4  2

This is a work of fiction. Names, characters, places, organizations, and incidents either are products of the author's imagination or are used fictitiously. Any resemblance to actual events, places, organizations, or persons, living or dead, is entirely coincidental.

For rats died in the street; men in their homes.

Albert Camus, *The Plague*

## PROLOGUE

One day, I asked my father what was the most distant city he'd ever visited. He simply said: 'Amsterdam, in the Netherlands.' And nothing more. Not looking up from his work, he carried on butchering dead animals. He had blood all over him, even his face.

When I wanted to know why he had made the trip, I thought I saw his jaw muscles tense. Was it the truculent hip joint of the veal haunch refusing to yield or my question that had set his teeth on edge? I didn't understand. There was a dull snap, then a sigh, and finally he said: 'To go fetch that dumb bastard Désiré.'

I had cut to the bone. It was the first time in my young life I'd ever heard him utter his older brother's name. My uncle had died a few years after I was born. I'd found photos of him in the shoebox where my parents kept photographs and Super-8 movies. In them you could see dead people who were still alive, dogs, old people who were still young, holidays at the sea or in the mountains, more dogs, yet more dogs, and family reunions. People in their Sunday best gathered for weddings whose vows would be broken. My brother and I would spend hours leafing through these photos. We'd laugh at the clothes people wore, try to recognize family members. Sooner or later, our mother would tell us to put them away, as though these memories somehow made her uncomfortable.

I had thousands of other questions for my father. Easy ones, like: 'To get to Amsterdam, do you turn left or right after the church?' Others more difficult. I wanted to know why. Why had my father, who never left the village, trekked across Europe to fetch his brother? But no sooner did a breach open in the dam holding back his grief and anger than he swiftly plugged it up, for fear of being completely engulfed.

Everyone in the family did the same when it came to Désiré. My father and grandfather never mentioned him. My mother always cut short her explanations, and always with the same words: 'It was all terribly sad, really.' As for my grandmother, she dodged every question with mindless euphemisms, with stories of the dead people going to heaven and watching over the living here below. Each in their own way appropriated the truth. Today, almost nothing of the story remains. My father has left the village, my grandparents are dead. Even the village where it played out is crumbling.

This is a last-ditch attempt to ensure that something survives. It is a mixture of memories, half-finished confessions and documented reconstructions. It is the fruit of their silence. I wanted to tell the story of what our family, like many others, lived through in total isolation. But how can I put their story into my words without robbing them of theirs? How can I speak on their behalf without my point of view, my preoccupations, replacing theirs? These questions long prevented me from starting to write this. Until I realized that only by writing could I make sure that my uncle's story, my family's story, did not disappear with them, with the village. To prove to them that Désiré's life was inscribed into the chaos of the world, a maelstrom of facts, historical, geographical and social. And to help them to move beyond their grief, to step out from the solitude into which they had been plunged by sadness and shame.

For once, they will be at the centre of the map, and all the material that usually gets attention will be relegated to the margins. Far from the city, from the cutting edge of science and medicine, far from the politically committed artists and activists, there will finally be a place where they exist.

# PART ONE
*Désiré*

# MMWR

The *Morbidity and Mortality Weekly Report* published in the United States by the CDC (Centers for Disease Control and Prevention) in Atlanta, Georgia has few subscribers in France. They include Willy Rozenbaum, an infectious disease specialist at Claude-Bernard hospital in Paris. At thirty-five years old, with his motorbike, his long hair and his past as an activist in Nicaragua and El Salvador, he cuts a curious figure in the medical community in Paris.

On the morning of 5 June 1981, he is thumbing through the *MMWR* that has just landed on his desk. In it, there is an account of pneumocystis pneumonia, an extremely rare lung infection. It was assumed to have been almost eradicated, but, according to the American service that records dispensing rates for medications, it has made a sudden, almost unbelievable resurgence. While pneumocystis almost exclusively affects severely immunosuppressed patients, the five cases recorded in California were young, previously healthy males. Of the scant details available to the American public health system, the article notes that, curiously, all the affected patients are homosexual.

Willy Rozenbaum closes the report and goes back to

his research work before spending the afternoon seeing patients.

That day, two men come to his surgery. They are holding hands. One of them, a gaunt airline steward, complains of a fever and a cough that has lasted now for several weeks. Since none of the doctors he has consulted have succeeded in treating him, he has come to the department of infectious and tropical diseases at Claude-Bernard. A puzzled Rozenbaum looks through the patient's medical file. He examines the young man before ordering X-rays and various pulmonary tests.

When the results come back several days later, they confirm what Rozenbaum suspected: the patient is suffering from pneumocystis pneumonia.

It is an extraordinary coincidence. The patient's every symptom precisely corresponds with what the doctor has read in the *MMWR*: this young, homosexual man with no reason to be immunosuppressed is suffering from an extremely rare pulmonary infection. It is right here, before his eyes. The same disease, one thought to have been almost eradicated, has been observed in six patients: five Americans and, now, one French man.

# THE STAGE SET

Flies. Flies everywhere. Flies on the cuts of meat, on the glass display cabinets. Black flies that stand out against the white tiles. Flies fornicating on pork chops and chicken thighs. Flies born in the folds of a rib roast that die, drowned in blood. Flies that delight in the hum of the compressor of the refrigerated display and laugh at the blue glow from the zapper intended to electrocute them. Flies that have conclusively triumphed.

This is pretty much all I remember about my grandparents' shop. The empty silence of a butcher's that has been deserted by most of its former customers. Those who still come do so to support the family in a last gesture of solidarity. They chat for a minute or two, more interested in gossip than in buying meat.

Today, nothing remains. A sign with the words *For Sale or Rent* and a telephone number is stuck over the shop window. The whole street has suffered the same fate. The greengrocer, the hairdresser, the bookshop, the haberdasher, the television repair service. All these shops have gradually been vacated, as have the apartments above. Since there is no one who wants to take up the lease, they have rolled down the shutters. Of the boom times, only one survivor remains on this death row: a little, quaint, outdated beauty salon. The street is hopelessly empty. The only living creatures are the stray cats that have taken over the cellars below the shops. They come and go through the broken grates and the ventilation shafts. Sometimes, a few teenagers hang out here. Perched on jerry-built mopeds, sitting on the steps of former shops, spending all day insulting each other and arguing over packs of cigarettes. In the space of a few decades, the once prosperous sous-préfecture has inexorably fallen asleep. What had been the centre is now a periphery. The children's cries have fallen silent. My stage set has vanished.

And yet, it could have great charm. With its plane trees lining the riverbank, its farmers' market, its winding alleys, you might almost think you were in a Provençal paradise. But, around the old village, the run-down council estates, the burned-out cars, the shuttered factories tell a very different story. To understand it, we must first establish the terrain: a small, forgotten town caught between two worlds, somewhere between the mountain and the sea, between France and Italy. Then, explain the topography: a village built in a deep valley where a stream meets a river on its last Alpine stretch before it disappears into the plains and dies in the Mediterranean. Next, describe the harsh climate, the winters that drag on in the steep gorges, the sweltering summers, as though it has chosen only the worst aspects of Alpine and Mediterranean climates. Between the dark pine forests swathed in mist and the oak groves of the sunny south-facing slopes, the village established itself as a market town where farmers from neighbouring villages came to sell their meagre harvest. Finally, we need to add some historical details, to remember that until the mid-nineteenth century this ghost town not far from Nice was still part of Italy. When the region was annexed, France made it a sous-préfecture in an attempt to instil a bond with its new country. The building of the trunk road and the railway line connecting Nice and Digne made it possible for the area to gradually emerge from its confinement. Colossal construction works, employing Italian labourers, bored the huge tunnels and erected the monumental viaducts that opened the way to the coast.

Despite a precarious economy, a small fraction of the populace managed to get rich, to accumulate assets: shops, businesses, land, apartments. A burgeoning middle class that lived cheek by jowl with the penurious farm and factory workers. On the black-and-white postcards of the early twentieth century, you can see these families proudly strolling along the promenade by the river, sitting on the terrace of the cafe on the town square. In one of the photographs from this period, you can see the pristine front of my family's butcher's shop A man in a suit is standing in the doorway, stiff and proud. His bow tie and his hat are immaculate. His name is Désiré. My great-grandfather looks seriously into the lens. There is a stark contrast between him and the other townspeople who are walking along the street in their dirty, patched work overalls. This single yellowing image says all there is to say about how much our name meant.

Until the early 1980s, the butcher's shop was still a thriving business. On Saturdays and Sundays, an orderly queue stretched down the street. For a whole section of the populace the place was respected and intimidating. The best cuts of meat and the choicest compliments were reserved for the well-heeled customers. Older cuts were palmed off on poorer families, those who scarcely dared cross the threshold and were not likely to complain. In the middle of the flourishing street of shops, we still ruled the roost. Not for much longer.

# THE ALERT

Jacques Leibowitch, an immunologist at Raymond-Poincaré hospital in Garches, is one of the rare readers of the CDC bulletins from Atlanta. In the early summer of 1981, his sister, a dermatologist working in Tarnier hospital, happens to mention that they have been treating two gay men for Kaposi's sarcoma, an extremely rare form of skin cancer.

On 3 July 1981, the *MMWR* ran an article with the headline 'Kaposi's Sarcoma and Pneumocystis Pneumonia Among Homosexual Men – New York City and California'. The report confirms the mysterious rise of these illnesses in young gay men in New York and California, and mentions that twenty-six American gay men have been diagnosed with Kaposi's sarcoma, four of whom are also suffering from pneumocystis pneumonia.

After reading the article, Jacques Leibowitch is doubtful. It is highly unusual for a medical review to define patients by their sexual orientation. But he also makes the connection with the two gay men suffering from the rare skin cancer some days earlier.

Rummaging among his archives, he finds an interesting file on a taxi driver of Portuguese origin who died in 1979.

The man died as the result of an unbelievable series of infections, in particular, pneumocystosis. All of this piques the curiosity of the immunologist, and he makes a couple of phone calls to major hospitals in the Île-de-France region. At Claude-Bernard hospital, he talks to a specialist in infectious diseases who has been asking the same questions. Willy Rozenbaum shares with him his initial observations. Through conversations with colleagues, he has identified five other recent cases of pneumocystosis that no one can explain. If he has managed to find six cases identical to those described in the *MMWR* in the space of a few weeks, there must be many, many more.

Faced with the inexplicable emergence of these two rare illnesses in France, the two doctors come to a conclusion: they have to sound the alarm.

# RUE DU 4-SEPTEMBRE

Bloody carcasses. For three generations, this had been the family gold mine. Hunks of meat sold over the counter in packages carefully wrapped in pink checked butcher paper and inscribed with the customer's name.

Legend has it that my grandparents got married at night to avoid the wrath of my great-grandfather. In the hope of protecting his heritage and his reputation, he had forbidden his children from marrying Italians. By the time they were of marriageable age, not one had failed to break this commandment.

I have often wondered how a secret night-time wedding could actually have taken place in a tiny village where everyone knows everything. I accept the romantic version of their story. I love it all the more because I remember them only as a couple completely wrapped up in their work.

They were never free of meat. Mondays were spent at the slaughterhouse and the other days tending the shop. They may have lowered the shutters in the early afternoon, but there were so many other things to do that they had a kitchen built in the back of the shop so they could eat lunch there. Despite the fact that they would only have had to walk three minutes from the rue du 4-Septembre to eat at home. The family house was nearby, just behind the church. It was known as 'the store', because it had once been used as a stockroom for the shop. Even their living space was defined by work.

The shop was closed on Sunday afternoons. But they had to make preparations for the week ahead: cut up the beef carcasses, salt the hams, coat the escalopes in breadcrumbs, marinate the pork snout to make brawn salad, produce tonnes of sausages using a hand-cranked mincer. This was followed by hours spent cleaning. The back of the shop was thoroughly sluiced: the walls, the floors, the machines, the knives, the vats in which the meat was transported. Diluted with soapy water, the dark crimson of the blood turned pink. A blade was scraped across the butcher's block to remove any meat embedded by the knife. It had been done so often that there was a hollow several centimetres deep in the huge carved wooden block. Finally, aprons and towels had to be boil-washed. Only for it all to begin again the following day. Shopwork dictated every minute of the day and offered no respite. Meat had given the family everything; we could not be disloyal.

My grandfather Émile also travelled hundreds of kilometres each week to supply the surrounding villages. His converted truck shuttled between the tiny hamlets that clung to the steep limestone slopes, stopping for a few hours here, a few minutes there. In these places where there had been no shops for years, people eagerly awaited his visits.

He knew the region like the back of his hand. His father,

Désiré, and his grandfather François before him had been dodgy dealers. They would buy cattle on the hoof for next to nothing from poor farmers, take them back and fatten them up on the hills outside the village. Once they reached maturity, the cattle would be slaughtered and the meat sold piecemeal at a comfortable profit.

People came to the shop because the meat was from cattle slaughtered by the butcher, a guarantee of quality. It was a specific qualification that I came across on Désiré's military service record, dated 1908: 'butcher licensed to slaughter'.

Gradually, the family had accumulated various holdings and they were now respected landowners.

Émile had spent his childhood here in the 1930s. At the time, it was a thriving little town, with hotels, laundries, a tannery and factories making furniture and pasta. As soon as he completed primary school, he was brought into the business by his father and quickly proved himself invaluable. He would go with his father to neighbouring villages to buy livestock. Outside the villages, at the end of rutted dirt tracks, there were isolated farms. Désiré had taught Émile how to choose the animals, how to negotiate the sale, and how to load the stubborn beasts into the cattle truck. He had proudly shown him how to fatten, slaughter and butcher them. This is how Émile came to be a butcher. His life was inscribed in the path of his forebears, in the memory of these lands. When their parents died, the children divided their savings, the apartments and the land between them. Since Émile was the eldest, he naturally took over the butcher shop and 'the store'. He inherited the business, the profession and the life of his father.

The story of my grandmother, Louise, was rather more turbulent. She was born into an Italian family in Piedmont. Her father worked himself to death on a farm in San Firmino for a pittance that condemned him to penury. Along his back, bowed by the heavy loads, over his sun-scorched neck, and in the hollow of his calloused hands, something finally germinated. He and his comrades in misfortune had dreamed of better tomorrows.

Things had taken a nasty turn. The threat to Italian communists was quickly escalating. The steady progress of fascism, its humiliations and abuses, left him with no choice. One night in 1942, he was forced to take his wife and his children and flee. After several days spent aimlessly trudging south, they found refuge in a village in the Roya valley. The locals in this staunchly left-wing stronghold suggested they take over a ruined house. Shortly afterwards, Louise's father managed to get work as a day labourer on some of the neighbouring farms.

The influx of Italian families to the region after the First World War did much to stem the rural exodus and make up for the absence of those men who had never returned from the trenches. These poor immigrants were highly prized by local employers, whether farmers, builders or factory owners. During this period, it was the sweat and toil of Italian men that dug the steep gorges and built the lofty viaducts that would one day support the road and the railway line that connect the Alps to the Mediterranean. But, after the great depression of the 1930s, they found themselves accused of everything: of being dirty, of tolerating unsanitary accommodation, accepting paltry wages and even of having too many children. Louise accepted her place in this toxic atmosphere. Like her father, she quickly learned to make herself invisible, to lower her eyes and to bite her tongue when faced with the contempt of her employers, those families for whom she cleaned, or cared for children scarcely younger than herself. She never complained. Here, they were as poor as they had ever been, but at least she no longer feared that the Blackshirts would show up on the doorstep one night and leave her father for dead.

My grandmother rarely talked about this childhood during which she lacked everything. She never lingered over details, but she would sometimes mention the cold, the hunger and the prejudice. She still remembered the little house that was too cramped for such a large family. As a girl, she had spent years sleeping on the floor and eating nothing but polenta. She hated bland food and exorcized her past by cooking lavish meals. This was her revenge.

There was nothing in my grandparents' house that recounted her story. Only her mother, now almost a hundred, wrapped in a blanket and afflicted with Alzheimer's, served as a reminder of her past. Sitting in an armchair, almost stone deaf, my great-grandmother would spend hours muttering unintelligibly in a mixture of Italian and Piedmontese. She would sometimes wake up in terror when some scene from her childhood had visited her in dreams. She would scream and howl as she searched for her husband, her parents. This was Italy coming back, like those memories we try to suppress in the middle of the night. In an effort to calm her, my grandmother would recover her lost language for a few moments.

Louise had met my grandfather in her late teens. Every Saturday in summer, one of the villages in the valley would celebrate its patron saint by organizing a fête. After mass, a wooden statue would be carried through the streets, then a dance floor would be set up on the village square. Beneath the garlands of twinkling lights, Émile asked Louise to dance. Within a few short songs, their future had been sealed. Despite the reservations of Émile's father, they were married. Louise was quickly integrated into the well-heeled minority in the village. In this small community, certain family names were proudly emblazoned on shopfronts or on the trailer of a car. Others were marked by the infamy of an alcoholic father or by a mother unable to cope with the escapades of her numerous children. Louise was determined that her children would be a credit to the caste she now belonged to. One in which children were referred to by their Christian names, went to mass, played tennis and were constantly praised by their teachers. Unlike the children of poor families who wandered the streets and got nothing but beatings from the headmaster, who bellowed their surnames and had them kneel for hours in his office with a dictionary balanced on their heads.

My grandmother now had people working under her; this was one of the benefits of her new class. Children with intellectual disabilities were placed with my grandparents by social services, first Pierre and later Susanne. This was common practice in the rural hinterlands of Nice. Numerous families were awarded financial compensation, and, in addition, they had more hands to help out with the work.

In the shop and at home, Louise asserted her status. She shouted, belittled, issued orders to people who were meek and biddable. To this day, former customers of the butcher's shop still remember her caustic remarks if someone was impatient to be served. My grandmother had overcome everything: exile, hunger, cold and humiliation. She treated others as she had been treated.

In the course of this life without respite, Louise and Émile started a family. They had four children: Désiré, Jacques, Christiane and Jean-Philippe. According to the custom in many Italian families, the eldest boy was given his paternal grandfather's Christian name. This name was the legacy of one of the few soldiers from the village who had come back from the trenches, the grandfather to whom the family owed their life of ease. The eldest boy was expected to set an example, to follow in his parents' footsteps, to honour the name that his forebears had striven to make known throughout the valley.

# GAY-RELATED IMMUNE DEFICIENCY

In July and, again, in August 1981, the *MMWR Epidemiologic Notes and Reports* note 'an uncommonly reported malignancy in the United States'. The illness has already infected more than a hundred patients from San Francisco to New York. For the moment, no one has been able to identify precisely what is causing the collapse of the patients' natural defences. Initial analyses show a catastrophic failure of the immune system.

While waiting for greater clarity, doctors do the best they can to treat the numerous symptoms and conditions suffered by those who have been infected. Fevers, night sweats, weight loss, chronic diarrhoea and swelling of the lymph nodes are identified as early signs of the illness, before patients develop more serious conditions such as pneumocystosis and Kaposi's sarcoma. The syndrome has been diagnosed in one woman and a few heterosexual men, all of whom are heroin addicts. Given the number of gay men currently infected, this seems negligible.

The illness often seems to progress in the same way: a few early successes, some moments of apparent remission, before the immune system becomes so weak that patients succumb to the onslaught of subsequent illnesses. Since gay men make up a large proportion of those affected, researchers initially focus on their lifestyle. For a time, poppers, a stimulant popular in the gay community, are thought to be a cause. American researchers visit gay clubs to take samples, which they analyse in laboratories. The hypothesis is quickly abandoned.

'Kaposi's Sarcoma. The Mysterious Illness Affecting American Homosexuals'.

On 6 February 1982, *Libération* is the first French newspaper to publish an article about the disease. The whole piece is marked by statements that are 'unconfirmed' or 'uncorroborated'. The journalist has done his utmost to gather what little information is available. He quotes Willy Rozenbaum, who cared for the first French cases at Claude-Bernard hospital, and gives the phone number of an 'epidemiological surveillance centre', which is simply the clinic of a Paris doctor.

Willy Rozenbaum and Jacques Leibowitch are utterly alone. Their colleagues mock their new patient lists and question the point of spending so much time and energy on an unknown illness that currently affects only a dozen or so people in France. There is little interest in researching this acquired immune deficiency.

On 6 March 1982, *The Lancet* publishes an article written by Willy Rozenbaum and five other doctors, 'Multiple Opportunistic Infections in a Male Homosexual in France', in which they describe the progress of the disease in the first patient to be identified by Rozenbaum on 5 June 1981. The young airline steward suffering from pneumocystis pneumonia quickly deteriorated and developed a number of infections, including, the following August, cerebral toxoplasmosis.

In December 1982, the *MMWR* publishes an article stating that Acquired Immune Deficiency Syndrome has been diagnosed in three heterosexual haemophiliacs and a baby who received a blood transfusion. Week after week, in publication after publication, the lists include more patients who are heterosexual, haemophiliacs, drug users, women and young children. But in France, as in the United States, the authorities cannot understand why a handful of doctors are so interested in what is still known as 'the gay syndrome'.

Willy Rozenbaum is now convinced that the syndrome is caused by a particularly aggressive virus that is capable of destroying the immune system, thus leaving young patients open to rare diseases. Based on the details of the initial patients, Rozenbaum believes that it is spread through sexual intercourse and through contact with blood. Rozenbaum and his colleague and friend, the virologist Françoise Brun-Vézinet, work by a process of elimination, considering all the recognized viruses that are transmitted through sexual contact and through blood. Cytomegalovirus – a herpes-type virus that chiefly affects people who are immunocompromised and can sometimes result in pneumonia – is a prime suspect. As senior virologist at Claude-Bernard hospital, Brun-Vézinet has previously studied the cytomegalovirus.

## SLEEPING CHILDREN

She knows how to detect it and she begins to analyse the blood and lymph nodes of the earliest patients. After a few weeks, the two doctors are forced to accept that, while cytomegalovirus is sometimes present in the samples taken from patients, it is far from universal. Cytomegalovirus is unlikely to be the cause of the syndrome.

They are probably dealing with a virus unknown to the researchers. Based on articles published in American medical journals, Willy Rozenbaum, Françoise Brun-Vézinet and Jacques Leibowitch begin looking into retroviruses. It is an appealing hypothesis, since there has been very little research into retroviruses, particularly in humans. The three French doctors lack the necessary expertise. They need help. Rozenbaum initially approaches Jean-Paul Lévy's team at Cochin hospital, only to be rebuffed. For his part, Leibowitch, who speaks fluent English, makes contact with Robert Gallo, a virologist in the United States who became internationally renowned when he discovered the first human retrovirus, HTLV, which is responsible for certain types of leukaemia. Leibowitch believes that the American is perhaps the only person who can help him analyse the patients' blood more accurately.

Meanwhile, Willy Rozenbaum's efforts to alert the media are beginning to bear fruit. Saturday, 27 March 1982 sees the first television report on the eight o'clock news bulletin on Antenne 2. The newsreader, Christine Ockrent, opens by citing the alarming increase in a rare form of cancer, Kaposi's sarcoma, in the United States. Curiously, it would seem only to affect homosexual men. This is followed by the journalist's report: a picture-postcard collage of New York, skyscrapers, yellow cabs and NYPD officers precedes images of muscular young men dancing in gay bars, and a series of vox pops in which worried passers-by complain that the only information they have been able to get comes from the handwritten posters in the windows of local pharmacies alerting the gay community to this new disease, with detailed descriptions and photographs of the classic symptoms.

Kaposi's sarcoma, the gay community: the stereotypes about those infected with the virus will remain unchanged for years, and, in the absence of any significant breakthrough, the media will simply broadcast images of the emaciated bodies of dying patients. Over time, the loneliness and isolation of those suffering from what is commonly known as 'the gay cancer' will only get worse.

Despite the fact that the news segment on Antenne 2 makes it clear that an increasing number of cases is being recorded in France, government bodies and the general public see the epidemic as a remote phenomenon. Willy Rozenbaum is struggling to broaden his audience. On a number of occasions, he tries to enlist the support of the association of gay doctors' association, only to be categorically refused. Some fear that their involvement would further stigmatize the gay community without fostering a greater understanding of the disease. Eventually, the association agrees to work with him to better identify and support those suffering from the disease.

In the hushed corridors of Paris hospitals, Willy Rozenbaum's vociferous concerns are beginning to unsettle people, something that will soon cost him dearly. One evening in May 1982, the axe falls. The director of Claude-Bernard hospital, embarrassed by the number of homosexual men attending Willy Rozenbaum's clinic, tells him that if he intends to continue working on this syndrome, he will have to find another hospital.

# BOYHOOD

My father never talked about that part of his work. Yet it was the basis of the family's reputation. Whenever I'd ask him to explain how it worked, he'd just say that you had to act quickly. Not because it was a complicated procedure, but because you didn't want to stress the animals. If you did, the meat would be spoiled. He used to say that cattle shouldn't have to suffer for nothing.

The breeder brought the first cow down from the truck. Lowing in the darkness, the others waited their turn. Leading the animal on a rope, the breeder guided it through a narrow path lined with metal barriers, whispering into its ear and patting it on the back to keep it calm. Pierre, the family 'employee', followed close behind. Émile and my father were waiting at the other end, in a huge white-tiled room in the glare of fluorescent tubes. Rails mounted on the ceiling were hung with hooks on which the cattle were bled out. When he reached the end of the lane, the breeder would jerk the rope, pinning the cow's head against the barrier. At this point, my father's knife would flash. Quickly, precisely. He would swiftly cut the carotid artery so the animal would die without a struggle, without even realizing it was being slaughtered.

This was better for all concerned. Once the bleeding was done, the animal was hung upside down to be gutted.

While the hanging carcass still shuddered with violent convulsions, my grandfather and father used their knives to cut away the organs. Then Pierre would push the eviscerated carcass along the rail and into the cold room, while the breeder went to fetch the next victim from the cattle truck. There could be no let-up, not until the last animal had been bled.

When the lowing finally subsided and the night was once more silent, everyone would troop outside for a break. Covered in blood and sweat, they would share bread and cheese and a flask of coffee under the stars. Sitting on the running boards of the cattle truck, they would trade news from neighbouring farms and villages. The local breeders congratulated the butcher who had taught his son to slaughter so well. This was why they came here: because their animals would be slaughtered better than anywhere else.

Sometimes, a yellow BMW with the radio blaring was parked between the trucks. The butcher's other son coming home from the coast. He'd spent the whole night partying. In his velvet suit and patent-leather shoes, he had been on a pub crawl with his friends through the seaside bars. The abattoir was located on the outskirts of the village, so he would stop off for coffee with his father before going to bed. Émile would proudly introduce his eldest son to the few farmers who didn't already know him. Désiré would light a cigarette and recount the night's escapades. Under his younger brother's admiring gaze and with his father's blessing, he would regale everyone until his audience had to get back to work. Then he would disappear, wishing good night to men who would not have one.

Désiré was the favourite son. This was often the case with brothers in the valley: the first son was spoiled; he enjoyed a special status, as though the individual attention he'd received before his brothers and sisters arrived never quite wore off. Émile was simply following his parents' example. Such things went unsaid, but my father, a second son, talked to me about them sometimes. He justified the way he had reared me and my brother, explaining how important it was that we were loved and treated equally. As though this had been the root cause of the tragedy. The way his parents had raised Désiré had become an example to be avoided. One day, when I refused to take the bins to the end of the street, claiming it was my brother's turn, he had a rare angry outburst. He told me about his childhood, how his parents always expected him to do the thankless chores they spared his elder brother: 'Désiré always had new clothes that couldn't get dirty, but since I only got his hand-me-downs, I could stack the wood in the garage, clean the back kitchen or take out the rubbish. When he put on a new jumper, I was even expected to carry his satchel on the walk to school!' Then, as he had said so often, he added: 'There are no favourites in my house.' Only much later did I understand the reason for this obsession, which, without saying as much, criticized his parents' style of childrearing and blamed them for his brother's fate.

At a young age, my father made himself indispensable in the butcher's shop. He was eager to please his parents and insisted on taking up his father's profession as soon as possible. Although he got excellent marks at school and his teachers encouraged him to carry on with his studies, he flatly refused. So determined was he that he got permission to leave school early. And so, at the age of fifteen, he gave up his boyhood in order to work. His whole life was consumed by the butcher's trade. He would get up at four in the morning and go everywhere his father went: to the slaughterhouse, to the shop, out on his rounds. While he was already living the life of an adult, his friends were going to school and spending their holidays partying. At Saturday night dinners, his eyes would close in the middle of a conversation. His head would gradually droop onto the table. Someone had to wake him for dessert. At first light, he would be up and out so he could be at the butcher's shop by dawn, when his friends were only just trudging home to bed. Little by little, he stopped talking about anything other than work and the hours he put in during the week. People called him a 'grafter', and this was his pride and joy. Customers, deliverymen and wholesalers praised his enthusiasm and envied his parents their devoted son. On Sunday afternoons, his shattered body would slump on the sofa. He would fall asleep watching American cop shows.

Meanwhile, his elder brother was discovering that a different life existed, far from the valley and the butcher's shop. The village school only taught pupils up to the age of fifteen, so Désiré went to study at Parc Impérial, a secondary school in Nice, setting off on the first train every Monday and boarding at the school during the week. Here, the cheerfulness and self-assurance fostered by a childhood lavished with praise and affection made him a natural leader. He was funny, high-spirited and made friends easily.

So, the eldest son moved into uncharted territory, filled with places and people known only to him. In the valley, his family were aware of everything that happened, but the greater part of his life was now being played out on a stage to which no one but he had access.

Désiré would come home on the Friday evening train. He would have dinner with his family then go to the cafe to meet up with his friends and tell them about his adventures in the big city. His parents had too much respect for his schoolwork to ask him to work in the butcher's shop at weekends. Besides, he didn't need to, since his younger brother already worked there. So, they simply told him not to do anything stupid. My uncle's freedom lay in escaping his family.

He was the first person in the family to pass the baccalauréat. For his mother, who had never studied beyond primary school, and his father, who had only a training certificate in butchery, the baccalauréat was a source of great pride. Désiré was impatient to be completely independent, so decided not to take his studies any further. The village solicitor was looking for a secretary. When Désiré showed up, he was hired on the spot. My uncle quickly moved into his own apartment, above the cafe on the village square.

Everything was going exactly as his father and mother had wished. Their eldest son had an education and a respectable office job. Their next son, the more practical and diligent, would carry on the business that had made their name.

# IN THE KINGDOM OF THE BLIND

Over the course of 1982, the number of patients diagnosed in France continues to rise. Willy Rozenbaum has found a job at Pitié-Salpêtrière hospital, where he can once again see patients. None of them have seen any improvement in their health. Deaths are piling up.

Infectious disease specialists are accustomed to dealing with death, but in these cases, patients are condemned twice over: to social as well as physical death. Newspaper articles and TV reports about the disease have spread fear throughout the population. Few family members are at their bedsides; patients are reduced to their sexuality, their drug use, and most have only a few doctors to talk to.

In the new hospital, Willy Rozenbaum becomes friends with David Klatzmann, a young immunologist, still a student, who helps him analyse patients' blood samples. Klatzmann confirms that, as has already been reported in some American publications, in the advanced stages of the disease, T4 lymphocytes are barely detectable.

On 27 July 1982, in Washington, the acronym AIDS (Acquired Immunodeficiency Syndrome) is formally adopted as the name for the disease. The name may have changed, but the stigma attached to what was formerly called 'the gay syndrome' has not.

Since spring, some twenty doctors have been meeting every fortnight in Paris, at the instigation of Willy Rozenbaum and Jacques Leibowitch. They include Françoise Brun-Vézinet and her pupil Christine Rouzioux, virologists at Claude-Bernard hospital, immunologists Jean-Claude Gluckman and David Klatzmann, pneumologist Charles Mayaud, psychiatrist Didier Seux and various specialist practitioners. They share observations from their work on the ground and develop hypotheses to dispel the shadows still surrounding this bizarre syndrome. Patients need better support. Representatives of the French Department of Health begin to attend the meetings, among them Jean-Baptiste Brunet.

The members of the French AIDS Working Group (known as the GFTS: Groupe français du travail sur le SIDA) are all young, the oldest barely forty. Only two are qualified professors; some have not yet finished their studies. None are medical or scientific heavyweights. The renowned specialists and doctors of the time have no interest in AIDS, which affects very few people, who, incidentally, happen to belong to sectors of the population considered marginal. These two points – the absence of leading medical figures and the fact that most patients are gay – mean that the GFTS is working in a climate of indifference.

The GFTS team is also remarkable in that it is multidisciplinary. As a rule, research specialists confine themselves to their specific field. Here, infectious disease specialists, immunologists, dermatologists, a pneumologist, virologists, a psychiatrist and general practitioners pool their knowledge. Representatives of the gay doctors' association also provide a link to the community worst affected.

At the group's first meeting, Willy Rozenbaum and Jacques Leibowitch present the case histories of patients they have identified, describe their symptoms and advance the hypothesis that this is a virus spread through sexual relations and contact with blood. They give an update on their initial exchanges with the CDC in Atlanta. The team drafts a press release to be distributed to as many doctors as possible in order to help identify further patients.

Jacques Leibowitch gives an account of his conversation about retroviruses with American virologist Robert Gallo. Leibowitch finds the notion that the disease is limited to male homosexuals extremely tenuous. He points to cases of Kaposi's sarcoma and pneumocystosis seen in female patients both in France and in the US. He also shares with his colleagues a ten-page memo he has written to alert the major French hospitals.

One of the first major tasks is to gather as much information as possible on the ground. Details of the symptoms are sent to hundreds of doctors, requesting that they report any potential cases they encounter. Once again, this initiative is met with indifference. By the end of 1982, there are only twenty-nine recorded patients, almost all of them in the Paris area, although the group suspects there are many more. Many doctors believe that the days of major epidemics are past, and few are willing to explore this uncharted terrain. A one-eyed man in the kingdom of the blind, the GFTS strives to understand what is happening, in a medical community that refuses to face the truth. Discussions are often heated. Jacques Leibowitch is prickly and often quick-tempered. Before long, he distances himself from Willy Rozenbaum and decides to work with Professor Gallo. In 1982, the first two French researchers to grasp the seriousness of AIDS go their separate ways.

At about the same time, telephone lines are set up to help identify and contact patients, both to offer information and also to learn from them. At this point, patients often know more than the doctors and play an important role in determining care plans by observing their own symptoms and sharing their findings. These young people, most of them men, are the same age as those caring for them. Many have been shunned by their families, who no longer want to touch or even see them. In the GFTS, many find the compassion and hope they thought they had lost.

# AMSTERDAM

*Amsterdam's a beautiful city. The people are lovely.*
*Be home soon.*
  *Much love,*
  *Désiré*

All the family's troubles began with these few words written on the back of a postcard received one morning at the butcher's shop.

On a whim, Désiré had given up everything. Some months earlier, at the local camping ground, he had got to know a group of Dutch students. My uncle was fascinated by the ease with which these young people travelled around, making friends along the way. They smoked a couple of spliffs and talked for hours. One of the couples, Annekatrien and Nell, gave him their address in Amsterdam and invited him to spend a few days with them when he had a chance.

There followed long, tedious shuttling between the solicitor's office and his apartment over the cafe on the square. Then, one morning, Désiré could not summon the energy to go to work. He packed a few things into a rucksack, popped into the butcher's shop while his father was having his afternoon nap and pinched some money from the till, went to the tiny village station and took the Autorail to Nice, and, from there, caught the night train to Paris. For the first time, at the tender age of twenty, he began to venture beyond the boundaries of a life that had felt like a prison. As the train hurtled on through the darkness, he felt increasingly free.

The day after his departure, the phone rang in the butcher's shop. The eldest son announcing that he was going to Amsterdam to visit friends. That there was no need to worry. My grandmother would have been unable to point out Amsterdam on a map. Before she had the time to tell him he had to come home right now if he was to keep his job, the call was cut short by the coin-operated phone. The meaningless drone of the receiver reminded her of her helplessness.

Her eldest son was off exploring Amsterdam. While the couple who had invited him were at university, he would wander the banks of the canals, the parks and the streets between Centraal Station and Dam Square. He melted into the crowd of hippies, punks and besuited office workers. Far from the village and his mother's watchful eye, the world seemed boundless. Between the money he had managed to save and what he had stolen from the till, he would be able to last a few weeks. When he ran out of money, he planned to go home.

One evening, as he was sitting waiting for Annekatrien and Nell in a bar downstairs from their apartment, a slim young girl with dark hair started chatting to him. She had noticed he hadn't eaten his peanuts and offered to take them. Seeing the way she wolfed them down, my uncle burst out laughing. In a muddle of English and French, they got to know each other.

Her name was Maya, she had just turned sixteen and had run away from boarding school. She had been sleeping rough for several days, and would come here in the evenings to buy a drink with the few coins she had managed to scrounge and gorge herself on the plates of peanuts the waiters set out on tables. My uncle told her the story of his life, the village, the monotony, the need to hit the road, the longing to live a different life from that of his parents. Maya instantly fell in love with Désiré, with his long dark hair and smouldering looks of Patrick Dewaere. The following day, Maya brought her few belongings round to Annekatrien and Nell's apartment: some clothes, a few Gerry Rafferty records and a battered guitar.

Back in the village, my father carried on working, as he always did. Before the butcher's shop opened, he would drop into the cafe to chat with the regulars, and read *Nice-Matin*, poring over the 'Valleys' section dedicated to news from what the city folk of Nice called the *arrière-pays*, the hinterland. On that particular autumn morning, the front page of *Nice-Matin* showed the bodies of two young boys discovered in the toilets of Nice train station. They had probably died of a heroin overdose. A few years earlier, according to the article, a seventeen-year-old girl had been found dead with a syringe in her arm in Bandol casino. That earlier case had made the front pages of the national press. It had led to the passing of a law that branded drug users criminals who could be sentenced to lengthy prison terms.

In the early 1970s, France had finally agreed to cooperate with the United States to eradicate 'the French Connection', the network importing morphine base from Turkey into Marseille and synthesizing it into heroin for the export market. American police and their French counterparts had expected to uncover an industrial-scale operation; instead, they found a plethora of tiny laboratories in modest houses in the *arrière-pays* of Provence and the Côte d'Azur. The vast organized 'network' turned out to be a fantasy; the reality was a handful of home laboratories housed in the bathrooms or garages of houses in Marseille, Toulon, Nice, Aubagne and Saint-Maximin.

France prided itself on having put an end to the heroin trade. According to *Nice-Matin*, since the tightening of legislation in France, production had simply moved to the Netherlands and Italy, which were now plagued by addiction. The article in *Nice-Matin* suggested that the heroin which had claimed the lives of the two boys found in Nice train station had probably come from abroad. In the village, no one seemed particularly concerned by this remote news story.

For my grandmother, time hung heavy at the butcher's shop. She browbeat her youngest: 'What on earth could he be doing there? Didn't he tell you anything? He's been gone three weeks now.' Meanwhile, her eldest son was enjoying his holiday at the far end of Europe. Why so far? Why Holland? After much pestering, my father probably told her that in Amsterdam it was legal to smoke marijuana, a substance you mixed with tobacco to get high. My grandmother, who had never touched a drop of alcohol or smoked a cigarette, would have been devastated by this revelation. What would the neighbours say if they found out her son was taking drugs? He had to come home. The family reputation was at stake.

My uncle's postcard had just arrived. On the back of the envelope was a handwritten address, care of someone named Annekatrien, in Amsterdam.

# PASTEUR

At Pitié-Salpêtrière hospital, Willy Rozenbaum and his colleagues at the GFTS are doing everything they can to further their knowledge of AIDS. They are undeterred by the prevailing climate of indifference. They are not prepared to abandon patients for whom they represent the last hope of care and compassion. They are appalled by the discrimination their patients increasingly face and by the grim fate society has reserved for them. They cannot bear their patients to be the subject of crude rumours. It has never occurred to Willy Rozenbaum to give up the fight. The research he has been conducting for more than a year is about to take a decisive turn.

Jacques Leibowitch and his American colleagues have persuaded him: what he is dealing with is a retrovirus. The infectious disease specialist does everything in his power to be allowed to present his work at the Institut Pasteur, where he believes he may find scientists with the skills necessary to conduct research in this field. He spends his evenings collating the data he has accumulated over the weeks. He needs to persuade the prestigious institute to help him.

On an autumn evening in 1982, the presentation being given in a tiny meeting room by an outside practitioner on a recently identified syndrome attracts only a few researchers from the Institut Pasteur. But Willy Rozenbaum is not discouraged. He painstakingly details what has happened over the past eighteen months: the first article in the *MMWR*, the first cases of pneumocystis pneumonia, Kaposi's sarcoma, the devastated immune systems, the increasing number of patients at his clinic, the GFTS meetings, their contacts with American researchers, the retrovirus hypothesis. He also emphasizes how society has treated these patients. His listeners seem wary. At the end of the presentation, he asks whether there is a retrovirologist in the room who might help him solve this riddle. No answer. The indifferent audience files out of the meeting room. Willy Rozenbaum has hit another brick wall.

At home, he gets a phone call from Françoise Brun-Vézinet asking how his presentation went at the Institut Pasteur. The young woman still runs the virology laboratory at Claude-Bernard hospital, where she continues to analyse blood samples, searching for the cause of this disease. Rozenbaum tells her it was a failure. She insists: there must be a team at the Institut Pasteur with the requisite skills. As a medical student, she attended lectures given by members of the institute and vividly remembers one virologist, Jean-Claude Chermann, giving a presentation about the results of his research into retroviruses. So, before she hangs up, she urges Willy not to give up hope, to carry on informing and alerting, and suggests that he get in touch with Chermann's superior, Professor Luc Montagnier, director of the institute's viral oncology unit.

# THE JOURNEY

When he had barely turned eighteen, my father was dispatched to bring his elder brother home from Amsterdam. The second eldest son had just passed his driving test and had bought his first car, a Golf, almost new. Most importantly, he was the one member of the family who always heeded his parents' orders.

I don't think I am aware of my father ever taking a plane or a train in his life. All he knew was his job behind the butcher's counter and the constellation of villages through which he and his father drove the butcher's van. He had never been travelling; he spoke no languages other than French and a smattering of the Italian dialect he used with his grandmother. These were the boundaries of his world. For him, the earth was still vast and largely unknown.

But this didn't matter. The second son of the family, the boy who would never let his parents down, was making plans to drive across Europe and find his elder brother. My grandfather gave him an envelope stuffed with cash and a road map bought from the local newsagent. My grandmother suggested he take his cousin Albert along with him. Albert and Désiré were close. Surely, he would find the words to persuade Désiré to come back. They set off for Amsterdam one morning with a scrap of paper scrawled with the return address from the postcard Désiré had sent to reassure his mother.

My father told me almost nothing about this trip. Although, to date, it is the longest journey he has ever made. It is my computer that provides me with the details of their journey. I now know that they turned right after the village church. One thousand, two hundred and eighty-three kilometres exactly. A drive of more than thirteen hours, not including rest stops. I imagine they took it in turns to drive and sleep. Digne, Grenoble, Lyon, Dijon, Nancy, Metz, Luxembourg, Liège, Maastricht, Eindhoven, Utrecht and, finally, Amsterdam.

The only thing I heard from my father is an anecdote he sometimes told to entertain friends who came to dinner. As they were driving into Amsterdam, they were stopped and asked for their papers. Seeing the green car and the green uniforms, they didn't immediately realize that they were dealing with police officers. Albert gave a dazzling smile and responded to their questions with insults in French. 'Every time one of the cops asked something in Dutch, that idiot Albert came out with some bullshit. And he found the situation so hilarious that he couldn't stop!' Realizing they were being insulted, the police hauled them in and they spent the night in separate cells, with bars in the ceiling through which snowflakes slowly fluttered. The following morning, they were released, frozen to the marrow.

I was fascinated by this story. My father had almost wound up in prison halfway across Europe and all for a stupid prank. This man I'd only ever seen behind the window of the butcher's shop. His life suddenly took on a surreal dimension. I wanted to know more, I tugged at his sleeve in front of the guests. But he carried on his grown-up conversation and promised to tell me another time. This story of his only foray into the wide world beyond the village was a point of pride whose memory he nurtured like a flame.

Although neither Albert nor my father spoke a word of Dutch, they managed to find Annekatrien and Nell's apartment in Amsterdam. Désiré was astonished to see them; all in all, he was pleased. He was sleeping on the sofa with a young girl he'd met a few days earlier. Maya insisted on going back to France with them. She had dropped out of school and was estranged from her parents. She wanted Désiré to show her France. It was she who persuaded him to go home. Not that my father gave his brother any choice. He couldn't imagine going back to the village and telling his parents that he had failed. Besides, my uncle was keenly aware of everything his mother had done to bring him home. He couldn't inflict such bitter disappointment on Louise.

They set out at dawn, all four of them. Albert and my father in the front, Désiré and Maya, an underage Dutch girl with no passport, in the back. The lovers had their pockets stuffed with weed, but everything went smoothly. They got to the village late that night.

The following day, Désiré introduced Maya to the whole

family. His father and mother were overjoyed to see him home and gave the girl a warm welcome, even if they were concerned about her age and her situation. Not only had their son trekked across the continent like a tramp, now he had also brought back a young girl who had run away from home. With Maya acting as interpreter, they contacted her parents, who did not oppose their daughter's decision and offered to regularize her position by filling out an application for her to be an au pair. A few days later, Émile and Louise drove Maya to Nice, where she applied for a passport and began the necessary formalities to be granted residency. This way, everything was legal and above board, and it would be easier to introduce her to the rest of the village. My grandmother's formidable facility for denial shifted into top gear. No, Désiré hadn't run off to Amsterdam without telling anyone. He'd been on holiday, staying with friends, and had brought back a young girl who was keen to learn French.

Maya and my uncle moved into his apartment above the cafe. She quickly became a part of the family and the bustle of the shop. Her first French words were butcher's terms. My grandfather taught her how to dress the shop window, how to salt and cure the cold meats. As there was little to do in the village, she would sometimes go with him up into the mountains. On Mondays, she would go to the slaughterhouse with him. To impress her, Pierre, the abattoir 'employee', would drink the steaming blood of the animals that had just been bled, before tossing the entrails to the dogs.

\*

My brother and I caught glimpses of this little hippie girl in photos from the period. In a random Polaroid, she and my uncle are snuggling on the velvet sofa in my grandparents' living room. Whenever we asked our mother who this strange girl was, she would smile and say: 'Oh, that's Maya, she was nice. She lived with us for a couple of months. She drank milk with her dinner. I'd never seen the like. She was a girl Désiré brought back from Amsterdam. Your father had to go and fetch him. There was a terrible fuss at the time.'

In another photo, Maya is sitting on the sofa next to Désiré, Albert and my father in a room with an orange carpet. This is the only surviving image of Amsterdam. Albert is pretending to drink wine from the bottle my father is holding. Maya and Désiré are laughing. My father looks really happy to be there. As though the trip had not been some difficult chore, but an opportunity to join his elder brother on the lam. A brief jaunt beyond the butcher's shop, with not a trace of the seething anger that would later erupt whenever I asked him about his brother.

# BRU

In early December 1982, Willy Rozenbaum manages to speak to Professor Luc Montagnier over the telephone. The director of the viral oncology unit at the Institut Pasteur listens attentively. This is an opportunity for the two men to review all the information they have about this new disease. Research has steadily advanced in France and in the United States over the past year and a half. There is now conclusive evidence that the disease does not only affect homosexuals. More and more cases are being reported in other sectors of the population: heterosexuals, heroin addicts and haemophiliacs. The disease is transmitted through sexual contact, and through blood. A significant proportion of those infected are Haitian, although no explanation for this has yet be found.

But AIDS is still largely unknown. All Robert Gallo's attempts to detect a virus in the blood samples of patients in the United States have met with failure. The pathogen appears to attack T4 lymphocyte cells, but so far it has proved impossible to identify. Given the numerous opportunistic infections that patients develop because of their immunodeficiency, it is difficult for doctors to get a clear picture of what is happening. One that might help them identify the cause of the syndrome.

One Saturday morning, an initial meeting is held at the Institut Pasteur to come up with a strategy. Willy Rozenbaum and Françoise Brun-Vézinet meet with three researchers: Jean-Claude Chermann, Françoise Barré-Sinoussi and Luc Montagnier. Given that it has proved impossible to detect the presence of a virus in patients in the advanced stage of the disease, it is suggested that they look for it in the early phase, before it destroys the immune system and erases all trace of its actions.

At Rozenbaum's suggestion, the members of the institute agree to study a biopsy of the lymph node of a patient in the earliest stage of infection. It is here that the pathogen embeds itself, and it is vital to select a patient who is on the verge of developing AIDS. Rozenbaum has a particular patient in mind, a gay man who has regularly visited the United States and has had numerous sexual experiences there. At present, he is suffering only from lymphadenopathy, an inflammation of the lymph nodes. He has few other symptoms, but Rozenbaum regards this as one of the first signs of infection. He has seen it in many patients who have gone on to develop AIDS. He asks the man whether he is prepared to take part in the experiment. Aware of the fate that potentially awaits him, the young man agrees.

On Monday, 3 January 1983, in an operating theatre, Willy Rozenbaum takes a biopsy. Late that afternoon, he gives a part of the sample to Françoise Brun-Vézinet. The sample is labelled BRU, a contraction of the donor's name. It is sent by taxi from Pitié-Salpêtrière to the Institut Pasteur in Paris.

Travelling in this little jar, at the bottom of the isothermal cooler being driven through the hectic traffic of Paris, may be the pathogen responsible for one of the deadliest epidemics of the late twentieth century.

# SLEEPING CHILDREN

This is probably how it began. In a slowly declining community, in the early 1980s. Children found unconscious in the street in broad daylight. At first, this was attributed to hangovers, alcoholic comas or a few too many spliffs. Nothing worse than their parents' generation had done. But people quickly realized this had nothing to do with booze or weed. These sleeping children lay with their eyes rolled back in their heads, one sleeve rolled up, a syringe hanging from the crook of their arm. They were impossible to rouse. A few slaps and a bucket of cold water were not enough. So, a group of passers-by would pick them up and carry them home to their parents, who relied on their discretion.

The older generation could not understand. These were the children of businessmen, of civil servants, the sons and daughters of shopkeepers, many of whom had amassed significant wealth. These were well-connected families with apartments, land, businesses. Their offspring were supposed to want for nothing. They had not had to fight in the Second World War, or the wars in Indochina and Algeria, had not endured the hardships, the hunger and cold. They had witnessed the 1968 student demonstrations on television, like some distant echo that faintly resonated in these remote valleys. While they had not personally taken part in the protest marches or the student strikes, they had benefited just as much from this challenge to ancestral authority. They were allowed to study, to live it up, to go astray even, if it meant finding their own path, far from the strictures of the world in which their parents had been raised. Already, their parents were imagining brilliant careers for them in local government or in major companies. Now here they were, in the early hours, sprawled lifeless on a pavement. Older villagers blamed the parents' lack of discipline, and the decline in traditional values.

Perhaps, quite simply, there was nothing to understand.

Legally, however, things were much simpler. Gendarmes would make unannounced visits to wealthy homes. Police cars would stand parked for hours outside ordinary homes where nothing ever happened. They would smash wardrobes, slash mattresses, rip open packets of food. Then they would dutifully inform the incredulous, outraged parents that their children were criminals. They would explain that, in accordance with articles L. 626 and L. 627 of the 1970 law aimed at combating addiction and drug trafficking, they were liable to receive prison sentences. Dealing, possession and using were lumped together indiscriminately. Regardless of the severity of the offence, their children ran the risk of up to ten years in prison. The law also made provision for addicts to be remanded to detox facilities. But in practice, the courts ignored these provisions, which they considered spurious. All those involved were simply treated as delinquents and criminals. It was this that really terrified their parents.

In a little village where everyone knew everyone else, a family's reputation meant a lot. But it carried little weight when faced with police officers. In the public prosecutor's office in Nice, parents no longer had access to a Rolodex of contacts they could call on to get the case dismissed or to intercede on their behalf. Once outside the valleys, they were out of their depth.

So, they tried their hand at negotiation. The children made solemn promises. They would never do it again. They would stop hanging out with the very people they grassed up for getting them involved in drugs. The foundations of evil had been laid. The children would lie. The parents would believe them. They turned a blind eye, ignored the evidence, cared more about what the neighbours would say than about the consequences for their children's minds and bodies. Theirs was a simple strategy: hold on and wait for things to blow over. Those who were truly worried sent their children to a clinic on the coast and paid for a detox programme. And, when they were clean, when they came back to the village, they would end up hanging out with the same people, and they would inevitably relapse.

Parents were in a state of shock; they could not understand, let alone react. They were bewildered. Some barely knew that cannabis existed. The more streetwise were asking questions to which they had no answers. Who started this thing? Where did the stuff come from? Who had sold it to their daughter? Who had shown their son how to shoot up? Where were they getting all this money?

The police had noticed an increase in robberies in the valley.

## SLEEPING CHILDREN

The hilltop villas, the local grocer's shop and the pharmacy had all been burgled. In the morning, motorists would find their cars stripped of radios. In the local cafe, people were quick to point the finger at young people from the working-class districts of Nice. Some even claimed to have seen Arabs loitering in the village. These accusations were quickly belied when the culprits were arrested red-handed. Those involved were local teenagers, children from the village.

When faced with the devastated families, the police would sometimes try to explain. Heroin smuggled through the port of Marseille had ravaged cities in America, and later it spread to other areas, from Paris and the Netherlands, sometimes from Italy. It was difficult to know from where exactly. It spread from town to village, from student clubs to small parties. It had made its way to the valleys via the teenagers studying at university in Nice who came home every weekend. The needle had replaced the spliff, and more and more people were eager for new experiences. The prime customers for dealers were these bored teenagers who were mesmerized by life in the city, and these same teenagers turned to dealing to fund their own habit. The greater the transgression, the greater the thrill.

Parents found themselves trapped in their private agony. They were almost out of their minds. They had spent decades working their fingers to the bone in the hope of a little comfort and respect. The hardest part was done. All that remained was for their children to take over some business tailor-made for them. Yet, in the gutters of the most squalid alleys of the village, their children were throwing it all away.

# SCIENCE

On the night of 3 January 1983, the biopsy from Willy Rozenbaum's patient arrives at the Institut Pasteur. Luc Montagnier immediately sets to work, cutting the section of lymph node into thin slices which he will culture. These he then distributes to his colleagues and awaits their analyses. A few days later, a second sample arrives from a different patient: LAI.

Jean-Claude Chermann calls his team into his office. Researchers at the institute are accustomed to working with dangerous viruses, but no one has the faintest idea quite how dangerous this 'thing' might be. Chermann wants to get everyone's consent before proceeding with the experiments; he does not want to force anyone's hand. The response is unanimous: 'If you're doing this, we're doing it with you.'

This is the beginning of a long process. After three weeks of analyses, Françoise Barré-Sinoussi, one of Chermann's former students, detects reverse transcriptase. This is an enzyme that retroviruses use to invade a host. The young researcher notices that things are quickly changing in her test tubes. Not only has she confirmed the presence of reverse transcriptase; she notices that the death of CD4+

T cells is so rapid that it will soon be impossible to find anything in these cultures.

At an emergency meeting in Jean-Claude Chermann's office, a decision is made to add white blood cells to the cultures to keep them active, using blood from donors at the Institut Pasteur. If they cannot detect the cause of the disease, they will feed it in order to give themselves time to identify it.

Given this rapid cell death, the Pasteur team comes to the conclusion that the hypothesis of American colleagues may not be correct. On the other side of the Atlantic, researchers have proposed the idea that the pathogen responsible for the disease is probably a retrovirus of the HTLV type. If this were the case, cells would tend to multiply. But the cells in the cultures of the Pasteur team are dying en masse.

Some days later, while studying her cultures, Françoise Barré-Sinoussi once again detects the RT enzyme typical of retroviruses, this time in much greater quantities. She tells Jean-Claude Chermann. He informs Luc Montagnier, who sends the samples to Charles Dauguet, the electron microscopist at the Institut Pasteur, who is trying to detect a retrovirus. Like the others, he has been made aware of the dangers of the work, but he is accustomed to analyses of this kind. Using cutting-edge technology, he examines every particle of the samples supplied to him. Conscious that the team may be on the verge of a breakthrough, Luc Montagnier comes by every evening to see whether Dauguet has detected anything. On 3 February, after an interminable week, his telephone finally rings. The microscopist is brief: 'Eureka, I can see it, I've got it!'

The whole team rushes to his office. Each in turn looks into the electron microscope to see a budding virus particle with its own morphology. It looks like nothing they have ever seen before.

It is not the HTLV virus, as Professor Robert Gallo has assumed. The virus identified at the Institut Pasteur is different. Its tendency to kill infected cells has been confirmed. A sample of the French virus, isolated from the lymph node of patient LAI, who was at a more advanced stage of the disease than BRU, is sent to the teams in America so that they can study it themselves.

On 20 May 1983, the prestigious American academic journal *Science* publishes an article reporting on the discovery by a team of French researchers of a deadly new virus that is probably responsible for Acquired Immunodeficiency Syndrome. Luc Montagnier prudently names it LAV, an acronym for Lymphadenopathy Associated Virus. It is important that the team distance themselves from the American hypothesis without claiming victory too quickly. The causal link between their discovery and the development of the disease has yet to be established.

# SUPER-8

It is a late spring morning in the countryside. We see people in their Sunday best walking around with movements made jerky by the speed of the film. They are having drinks outside a little house. There is probably the sound of laughter, gravel crunching underfoot, birds singing and the wind rustling though the leaves. But my father's camera could not record sound. So, everyone is silent. All we can hear is the clatter of the projector that has turned these people into ghosts.

People pass around two identical babies and pose with them for the camera. Children chase each other while the grown-ups drink and dogs surreptitiously steal crackers. Unusually, my mother's and my father's families are together on this reel of film wrapped in yellow Kodak paper, on which someone has written 'Twins' Christening'.

At one minute, thirty-two seconds, in one corner of the picture, we see a couple in the background, a man and a woman, who look a little out of it. Their emaciated bodies, haggard faces and loose teeth make them look like skeletons. They look so alike anyone would think they were brother and sister. Désiré and his wife Brigitte are already strung out on heroin. It's so obvious it burns through the screen; only my grandmother couldn't see what everyone else had realized some time ago.

Désiré and Brigitte had met some years earlier, a few months after Maya left, at a party in Nice. She was the only daughter of a wine rep who spent all his time on the road. His wife and his daughter had spent most of their lives waiting for him to come home. After years of neglect, the mother filed for divorce and she and Brigitte went to live with one of her sisters in a little flat in the north of the city. With her time taken up by her secretarial job and her disastrous private life, her mother allowed the barely teenaged Brigitte a lot of freedom, especially since her daughter's friends included a cousin whom she trusted completely. These were working-class kids from the underprivileged area of the city, light years away from the postcard images of the Côte d'Azur. They could be seen wearing black jackets, riding motorbikes around the neighbourhoods of Madeleine, Pasteur and Las Planas. Far from the palm trees, the bright lights of the beaches and the hilltop villas, these kids wore out the seat of their jeans in deserted squares, on patches of waste ground converted into supermarket car parks, and the shadows of slip roads. A lot of boys and a handful of girls who made their living from casual work, unemployment benefits and shady deals. Having spent a lonely childhood waiting for a father who never came home, Brigitte clung to them the way you might cling to a motorbike rider, praying he will take you far away.

After their first meeting, Désiré often bumped into her at parties up in the hills, or spending her afternoons in dive bars. After a few months, Brigitte came and settled in the village, where she was immediately hired as a care assistant in an old people's home. Although there were very few jobs in the valley, the work here was so gruelling and the churn rate so high that anyone could just walk into the job without a single qualification. To distinguish them from the secretarial and nursing staff, they were known as 'arse-wipers'.

In the thirty or so home movies in my father's collection, Désiré and Brigitte appear only once more. A Super-8 reel in a box whose title has been erased by time. Shot from the rose garden in the monastery on the top of Cimiez hill, the camera looks down over Nice. The sky is low and grey. In it, my father's family looks happy. Jean-Philippe, the youngest of my uncles, is grinning as though someone has just told a joke. Parked outside the gates of the rose garden is a line of old-fashioned cars. Brigitte, wearing a little white wedding dress, steps out of one. Standing next to my grandmother, wearing a burgundy suit and bow tie, Désiré is waiting for her at the far end of the gardens. They are not gaunt, nor do they look out of it. They have not yet lost their teeth. They have not yet retreated to a corner of the picture. They are still among the living. They look happy; it is a shy happiness, but they are happy nonetheless.

When the flickering image abruptly vanishes from my bedroom wall, I realize that they could have had a life away from drugs. A life in which they might have been happy. A life in which I might have known them. A simple life, one that might not have been worth recounting, but a whole life. This is the day to which you'd need to travel back in time in order to start again, to do things differently. Now, only by watching my father's Super-8 films in reverse order is it possible to bring these people back to life.

# KINSHASA

Despite the considerable progress made in research laboratories from Paris to Washington, in 1983 public opinion is still that AIDS only affects three so-called 'at-risk' groups: homosexuals, heroin addicts and haemophiliacs. This is despite the fact that the *MMWR* recorded cases of AIDS in heterosexual women as early as 12 May 1982. There is a fourth group that, for unexplained reasons, is disproportionately affected: Haitians.

For a long time, the attention of researchers and the rejection of society will be focused on these 'four Hs'. They are all regarded with deep suspicion. This is unbearable for committed doctors like Willy Rozenbaum. Marshalling the energy that has been his driving force for more than two years, he continues to speak out and to advance the scientific understanding of AIDS. This is essential in combating the prejudices that have shaped public opinion.

At the Institut Pasteur, work to establish the causal link between LAV and AIDS is continuing. To prove that the virus does not only affect the 'four H' groups, it has to be detected in people from other groups. In mid-September 1983, Rozenbaum presents the case of a dying patient to Professor Montagnier. The young woman shows all the advanced symptoms of infection. Yet she does not fit into any of the groups in which they are normally found: she is heterosexual, and she is from Zaire. She has never used heroin and never had a blood transfusion. But she is dying of AIDS, Rozenbaum is convinced of this fact. He has followed enough patients over the past two years to be able to identify the typical symptoms.

With the patient's consent, he takes a blood sample and sends it to the Institut Pasteur. Luc Montagnier cultures the cells before sending samples to Jean-Claude Chermann and Françoise Barré-Sinoussi. Their laboratory has been responsible for tracking the virus discovered a few months earlier in blood samples. Their working process is now tried and tested. The results come back quickly. Before the end of September, Rozenbaum gets a call to his office at Pitié-Salpêtrière hospital. Montagnier is categorical: this young woman is definitely infected with the AIDS virus.

The two men are unsurprised, but for two reasons this news proves to be crucial. Firstly, it is tangible proof that the virus can be transmitted between heterosexual couples. Secondly, because the patient has only just arrived from Kinshasa. Like many of the patients identified around the world, she has spent time in Africa. While the disease can infect anyone, it has become increasingly clear that it is disproportionately present in major African cities.

## SLEEPING CHILDREN

Willy Rozenbaum never gets the opportunity to give the results to his young patient: she dies two days after her blood has been taken.

For researchers, the looming threat is ever more apparent: the possibility of a pandemic.

# COFFEE

It was a Sunday. It could only have been a Sunday. Such a thing could not happen on any other day of the week. My parents had invited my father's parents to the house for coffee. They wanted to be somewhere quiet, far from the responsibilities of the butcher's shop.

Since time immemorial, my father's whole world had revolved around family. He had left school when still underage in order to work in the butcher's shop that bore the family name. He still worked there, ever loyal, despite offers from various rivals, who knew him to be dedicated and hard-working. One day, a supermarket appeared on the outskirts of the village. My father applied to run the butcher's counter. He sailed through the interviews, patiently underwent the training sessions. Then, on the day the supermarket opened, he left them high and dry. As he had always planned to do. He went back to work for his parents. The other shopkeepers in the village complained that they were being ruined, that their customers were being stolen. But my father was not one to take things lying down; he fought back. He left the supermarket with a cold store full of meat and no butcher. He would have done anything for his parents' business.

But now, for the first time, with a single sentence, he was about to shatter their world. All the things they had spent decades building up: a thriving business, a hardworking family, well-educated children ... with a few words, all these things would be destroyed. And he would have to say them. As though it had been written. My mother had almost certainly offered to speak instead. My father had refused. He was determined to be dignified, to take it upon himself.

He had his parents sit down on the sofa. My mother placed the tray on the coffee table. After some small talk about the weather, work, the wallpaper, my father took the bull by the horns, not because he was particularly brave, but because he could find nothing else to say to postpone the fateful moment. The previous evening, and not for the first time, he had noticed that there was money missing from the till. He had counted and recounted, checked every receipt, but it did not add up. He already knew why money had been going missing. This was why he wanted to talk to his parents. He took a deep breath. It was Désiré. He had been stealing money from the till at lunchtime while the shop was closed.

My grandmother was incredulous. 'Désiré? Désiré sneaking into the shop between twelve and two to steal money from his parents? You don't know what you're talking about! Whenever you or Désiré needed anything, your father and I have always given it to you!' My grandmother could not believe it. Why would her elder son, a successful young man with the qualifications necessary to get a good job, need so much money? It made no sense.

Like a dam bursting, the words continued to pour from my father. Because Désiré was taking drugs. Because he and most of his friends were shooting up. Because heroin was ruinously expensive, and he constantly needed larger, more frequent doses, and was probably being overcharged now that he was hooked. My mother added that one night when they were round for dinner, Brigitte had stolen some jewellery of no particular value that she had inherited from her grandmother.

My grandfather sat, miserable and silent, while my grandmother worked herself into one of her towering rages. She could be heard at the far end of the village. 'She called us liars, that's how desperate she was not to believe that her son was taking drugs,' my mother told me one day. My grandmother said they were just jealous. The only explanation was that my father and mother were jealous of Désiré and Brigitte. Jealous of his success, his job, his car, his position. My grandmother demanded that my grandfather get up, and they went home. Louise's fury did not abate along the way.

Now I realize that the cash being stolen from the till represented much more than money. It represented years of training, apprenticeship and work, thousands of nights with little sleep, of getting up at the crack of dawn, of holidays endlessly deferred. The money was not just theirs; it was my father's. Désiré was not just stealing from his parents, he was stealing from his brother. In ratting his brother out, the younger son, still very much a child, expected his parents to support him. He expected some sign from them. Some indication that all his hard work had not been for nothing; something that might acknowledge the man he had become. This money represented his devotion, a son's love for his father and mother. A son who could have left them in the lurch and gone to work elsewhere, but had always been loyal. Now here they were belittling him in front of his wife so they could protect the image they had of their eldest son.

My parents were not particularly surprised. They had expected nothing else of the visit. My father had done what he believed was his duty as a son and a brother. One day, my grandparents' denial would come face to face with reality. The pasteboard backdrop they had constructed would not long survive the village rumours. The respect that they had worked so hard to gain would crumble when the police came with a search warrant. The silence would soon be broken by the wailing sirens of the paramedics who saved Désiré after his first overdose.

# ROBERT GALLO

Despite the findings of the research team at the Institut Pasteur, Robert Gallo is not prepared to admit that the virus that causes AIDS is significantly different from the first human retrovirus, HTLV-1, which Gallo discovered in 1980. It was this work that cemented his international reputation.

Unlike the members of the small multidisciplinary team in France, Gallo is a leading light in his field. He works with a much more influential body than that of his Parisian counterparts: the National Institutes of Health in Bethesda, Maryland. In Room 6A11, his laboratory at the top of Building 37, he remains convinced that the Institut Pasteur team accidentally contaminated their samples. The discovery of a new virus in Paris has come as a shock. He intends to set things right.

As a regular collaborator with the French researchers, he receives samples of infected cells from Jacques Leibowitch, based at Garches hospital. The biopsy is from a patient who was infected during a blood transfusion after a motorcycle accident in Haiti. Robert Gallo sets to work using this sample. He analyses the cells, searching for the virus he discovered, and, eventually, he finds it. He is categorical:

AIDS is caused by the HTLV virus. Triumphantly, he presents his results at seminar after seminar. A number of academic journals, including *Science*, publish articles in which he announces that he has isolated the HTLV retrovirus in patients' blood samples, casting doubt on the French discovery.

What Robert Gallo does not yet know is that the transfused patient on whom he is basing his claims was doubly infected: by the HTLV virus, which is widespread in Haiti, and also by the AIDS virus. This unfortunate coincidence leaves Gallo trapped in a rut and, with him, a large part of the international community, who have more confidence in the work of the eminent American scientist than that of a small group of unknown French researchers.

# THE SECRET

After my grandmother had recovered from the shocking news, without admitting as much to my father, she decided to consult the elderly village doctor. In a village where everyone knew everyone else, this was particularly difficult. The doctor's surgery was on the ground floor of a decrepit old building, in a dark alley that stank of cat's piss. At the end of a dimly lit hallway, people patiently waited their turn amid the groans and whispers of the poky waiting room. After they had leafed through the dog-eared magazines on the coffee table, they stared vacantly at the only two pictures on the wall: an anti-smoking poster and a reproduction of a painting from the Middle Ages. The painting depicted a naked young woman with a sheet draped over her breasts and her genitals, flanked by two black-suited doctors in pointed hats, each holding a syringe so huge that, as a boy, I wondered whether people were supposed to take the image seriously.

In the privacy of the consulting room, seated beneath a wooden crucifix, the doctor adopted the tone of a moralistic parliamentary report. He blamed intellectuals, newspapers, books and rock music for being lax about drugs and bragging about their experiences to young people. Such messages caused even greater devastation in the countryside, where young people often lacked the self-confidence to say no. The elderly man lashed out at city folk, at a society that no longer set boundaries, at the unwarranted freedom given to children which, he believed, left them vulnerable to deep-seated anxieties, leading them to blame themselves.

He went on to tell Louise how heroin had gradually spread from the young people in coastal cities to those in the valley. The drugs units in the hospitals in Nice were so overwhelmed that most addicts were sent to Sainte-Marie psychiatric hospital. This was the only place where their cravings could be controlled with straitjackets and tranquillizers. But drug rehabilitation programmes were not enough. Various local initiatives had been launched in an attempt to deal with the problem. Michel Zavaro, a public prosecutor in Nice, was sick and tired of seeing the same addicts show up at his chambers every Monday charged with mugging people and stealing car radios. He had set up a specialized centre in one of the villages where drug addicts fresh out of rehab treatment were offered a stable environment and useful activities. With the exception of a handful of success stories, most residents ran away and relapsed, leaving the centre's staff exhausted. After four or five years, the project had been abandoned. The grip of heroin was too powerful.

As he walked my grandmother to the door of the

consulting room, the doctor told her that he had seen the damage caused by opium during the Indochina War. Opiates were by far the most addictive products he had ever seen. Any treatment would be long, expensive and difficult. The important thing was to be firm and keep my uncle away from the wrong kind of people. Louise asked him to put her son on a waiting list for a rehabilitation centre. Now she had to get Désiré to agree.

# CRUSADE

Ultimately, the fact that the French have taken a decisive lead in research into the new virus is of little consequence as long as their work goes unrecognized by the international scientific community. Luc Montagnier, Françoise Barré-Sinoussi, Jean-Claude Chermann and Françoise Brun-Vézinet travel the world, attending conference after conference, presenting their research which proves that LAV, the virus they isolated at the Institut Pasteur, is responsible for AIDS. But they are far more skilled in the laboratory than they are at persuading large crowds. Especially since they lack the reputation and the eloquence of Robert Gallo, who persists in defending the HTLV hypothesis.

In July 1983, Robert Gallo invites Luc Montagnier to the United States. Montagnier brings a test tube containing the French virus in a small isothermal cooler so that Gallo can study it for himself. Charming to a fault, Gallo goes to the airport in person to greet his colleague and invites him back to his home. Montagnier receives a warm welcome. It is Sunday. Gallo will not begin studying the Paris sample until Monday and so, much to his wife's dismay, he places it in the family freezer.

In the months that follow, there are further meetings and exchanges of data, but to no avail. Gallo and his team are convinced that the LAV virus is simply a cousin of HTLV, a point they hammer home in seminars, academic papers and conferences. They refuse to acknowledge that LAV is the pathogen that causes AIDS and impose their views on the rest of the scientific community. In France, the Pasteur team can only suffer in silence. They know that they will have to work harder, make greater strides, accumulate concrete evidence in order to convince them.

In Paris, at Willy Rozenbaum's instigation, Luc Montagnier meets with immunologist David Klatzmann and epidemiologist Jean-Claude Gluckman. They worked with Rozenbaum on the case of the airline steward who visited the Claude-Bernard clinic in June 1981. Together, the three men tried to work out the reasons for the young man's immune deficiency. Later, Klatzmann and Gluckman would participate in the first meetings of the AIDS working group set up by Rozenbaum.

Their current objective is to find irrefutable proof that LAV is responsible for the disease. To do so, they need to understand how the retrovirus attacks the immune system. Once LAV has been conclusively linked to AIDS, there will be no room for doubt. This is why Jean-Claude Gluckman and David Klatzmann have been invited to join the team at the Institut Pasteur.

On the other side of the Atlantic, Robert Gallo continues to play by the rules. To show that he is acting in good faith, he regularly invites his French colleagues to come and present their work alongside him at conferences.

On 14 September 1983, Luc Montagnier is invited to speak at a virology meeting hosted by the prestigious Cold Spring Harbor Laboratory, on Long Island. In a presentation lasting some twenty minutes, the French virologist outlines the findings of the Institut Pasteur. The American researchers, having already accepted the notion that the virus discovered by the French was probably the result of laboratory contamination, greet the presentation with scepticism and indifference. Montagnier, suffering from jet lag, and speaking in broken English with poor visual support, struggles to make a compelling case for the French discovery to counter the erroneous American hypothesis for which the red carpet has been rolled out.

But, on the very day of the meeting, the Institut Pasteur files a patent for its first screening test, the result of research carried out in parallel on antibodies from infected patients. The Franco-American battle over patents, rooted in an ambiguous mix of cooperation and competition, has only just begun.

# AT THE RIGHT HAND OF THE FATHER

Gradually, my grandmother's rage abated. My grandfather had even found his son unconscious in the street with a needle in his arm. It was impossible to ignore the truth any longer. For my grandparents the shock was so great that for a long time they were unable to talk about it. But at least they now knew. So, although they refused to discuss the subject, cordial relations with my parents quickly resumed, as if their argument about Désiré had never happened, since the work at the butcher's shop made it necessary.

It took Louise weeks, perhaps months, to admit what was happening. After her discussion with the village doctor, I imagine she finally came to terms with it, at least in her own mind. But when it came to keeping up appearances, she could not admit anything. My grandmother was only twelve years old when she and her family fled the war and Italy. She had spent her whole life avoiding the contempt of a society that long regarded her as an outsider. She had worked hard to shrug off her Italian heritage with a family of in-laws who had never approved of her. She had all but forgotten her mother tongue. She could not bear to lose everything. After so much effort, so many years, she simply could not bring herself to face up to the addiction of her son. Désiré, the pride of the family. The only one of her children who had studied in Nice, who had managed to get a good job in a solicitor's office.

From the indiscreet gossip of customers, she heard about other young people in the area who had been affected by the drug. The son of a businessman, or the daughter of a local councillor, found unconscious in the street or in some dingy apartment. The volunteer paramedics from the village were increasingly called out to deal with teenagers they knew well. More often than not, they had to be transferred to a hospital in Nice, leaving the village with no emergency services for hours.

My grandmother felt helpless. Her angry outbursts had no effect. In private, she begged her son to stop taking drugs. Désiré promised her a dozen times, a hundred times and more. It was enough. She needed to believe. Besides, the arms her son showed her did not lie. The track marks had begun to scar and heal. Already this nightmare was little more than a bad memory.

Then, one Sunday morning, while the shop was full of customers, the telephone rang. It was the mother of one of Désiré's friends. She sobbed as she repeated what her son had just told her. Despite his promises, he was still taking drugs, and so was Désiré. They had shifted to injecting between their toes or into their thighs.

Finding herself backed into a corner, my grandmother once again let anger get the better of her. This woman's accusations had taken her back thirty years, and she was once again the little immigrant girl that people looked down on, the girl who was expected to lower her eyes in front of village worthies, the girl who felt ashamed. Whenever my grandmother experienced something that reminded her of her childhood, she flew into a rage. Her screams could be heard far beyond the butcher's shop. Her son didn't take drugs! He had never taken drugs! Just because this woman's son was an ill-bred lout didn't mean that Désiré was one – far from it. Embarrassed, my father and my grandfather carried on serving the baffled customers as though nothing was happening. Before my grandmother slammed down the phone, the caller just had time to mention that she'd had her son undergo a series of tests a few weeks earlier. The results had just come back: her son had contracted the AIDS virus. Since he and his friends frequently shared needles, Désiré should see a doctor. It was very important.

My grandmother went straight back to work. She called on the customers to back her up: 'Can you believe the cheek of these people? Just because their children take drugs doesn't mean everyone else's do!' Once again, precious time was spent in denial.

As the days passed, Louise was forced to face the fact that Désiré had not been able to give up drugs as easily as he'd claimed. But my parents did not dare broach the subject again until her fury had subsided. They almost certainly left it to my grandmother to start the conversation. The only way she could talk about such things was by downplaying her son's involvement in such sordid matters. She thought long and hard before finally accepting the truth.

One night, when the shop was closed, as my father was rolling down the shutters and my mother had just arrived, my grandmother sighed as she folded her butcher's apron and said: 'AIDS. Whatever next? Oh, I've no doubt Désiré and Brigitte get up to no good with that gang they're hanging out with, but even so, how could he possibly end up catching it?'

My parents had heard about AIDS on the news. It was spring 1983 and very little was known about it. It was serious, it was a death sentence, at least at that time. It had been diagnosed in the United States and in France. It mostly affected homosexuals, and sometimes heroin addicts. It was transmitted through blood. If Désiré had shared needles with his friend, then yes, he might be at risk. He had to go and see a specialist on the coast and persuade Brigitte to do the same.

My grandmother was still very much the matriarch of the family, but what was happening left her so stunned that she did not know how to react. She would go through long periods of denial followed by brief moments of lucidity, during which it was vital to get things done before she once again became paralysed for weeks.

Unable to deal with the situation any other way, Louise could only talk about it by resorting to ridiculous euphemisms, foolish nonsense that ignored the brutal, violent, cruel reality... In her words, addiction was 'misbehaviour', rehab therapy was 'resting', AIDS 'a condition' and, later, her dead son would be 'a star ascended to the heavens'. As though a heroin addict could end up seated at the right hand of the Father.

# FAILURE

On 23 September 1983, the team at the Institut Pasteur gives a strain of the virus to researcher Mikulas Popovic, one of Robert Gallo's chief colleagues. While Gallo is still insisting to anyone who will listen that AIDS is caused by a virus of the HTLV family, Popovic is studying the virus isolated by Montagnier's team in Paris.

On 6 October, he goes to Gallo's office to tell him the results of his work. His results are categorical. The virus isolated by the Institut Pasteur is different. It does not belong to the HTLV family. To make matters worse, it is *this* virus rather than HTLV which has been systematically found in patients with AIDS. It turns out that the initial samples on which Robert Gallo and his team based their hypothesis were doubly infected, by both HTLV and LAV. Popovic no longer has any doubts: HTLV is not the pathogen that causes AIDS. The French did not make an error. They did not mistake Gallo's virus for something else; they have discovered a completely new virus. For Gallo, it is a decisive failure.

Robert Gallo stubbornly refuses to back down. Rather than admit that what he is dealing with is not a virus from the HTLV family, he decides to name the virus discovered in the French samples HTLV-3. By renaming it in such a way as to cause confusion, he hopes not to lose control of the situation.

On 24 April 1984, at a major press conference, Margaret Heckler, US Secretary of State for Health and Human Services, announces that Professor Gallo's American team has definitively identified the virus responsible for AIDS: it is a retrovirus, named HTLV-3.

On 4 May, *Science* publishes articles by Gallo describing HTLV-3. They are accompanied by a number of photographs. Among them is a photograph of the LAV virus taken under the microscope at the Institut Pasteur in 1983. There is utter confusion.

Many scientists around the world acknowledge the work of French researchers in the results Robert Gallo is claiming as his own. There ensues a long and bitter controversy. Faced with the evidence, Gallo will eventually claim to have 'inadvertently' used the sample. Given what was at stake financially from the first screening tests for AIDS, many found this hard to believe. The working notes of Mikulas Popovic, published some time later, leave little room for doubt on this point.

# THE NEW PLAGUE

Blue lesions on skin and mucous membranes, mouths spewing pink, blood-flecked foam, corpses hastily piled up in the corridors of an overtaxed intensive care unit – it was not something that Professor Dellamonica was likely to forget. Before he even completed his studies, Dellamonica experienced his first medical nightmare in the emergency department of Édouard-Herriot hospital in Lyon. Hong Kong flu, which suddenly arrived in Europe from Asia in the winter of 1968, left numerous French hospital wards overwhelmed, before disappearing just as abruptly. For Dellamonica, this baptism of fire left a lasting impression. Throughout his career, the infectious disease specialist would remain deeply humble in the face of viruses. After completing medical training, Dellamonica moved to Nice, where he ran the department of infectious diseases at L'Archet hospital. In the early days of Franco-American discoveries concerning AIDS, he too had embarked on a programme of research. He had questioned fellow practitioners, reopened old patient files from the pneumology and dermatology departments and identified a number of patients who had died of unusual infections. His interest in a syndrome that affected only homosexuals and drug addicts earned him the scorn of colleagues. But he had persisted in his research, believing that it was his duty.

Less than an hour's drive from the village, we were no one. Our name meant nothing; even the name of the village conjured only images of some remote, backward outpost. Whenever we went to Nice, we always made a sartorial effort. We made sure that our clothes were freshly pressed, our shoes polished, our hair neatly combed. To no avail. Everything about us – our way of walking, our manners, our vocabulary, our expressions – gave us away. I can't imagine that it was any different when my grandparents took their eldest son to hospital: they probably looked like hayseeds, dressed in their Sunday best, desperately waiting to see a doctor. Rednecks sitting whispering in the corridor outside the surgery of a renowned specialist in infectious diseases.

When, finally, they were sitting in his office and he asked the reason for their visit, it was my grandmother who spoke up. She finally had to speak. Far from the village, she tore down the walls she had erected to shield them from the terrifying reality. Here, the words 'drugs', 'heroin' and 'needles' elicited no disapproval from the doctor. Not so much as a raised eyebrow. Looking into Dellamonica's blue eyes as he listened dispassionately to her story, Louise gave up the role she had grown used to playing. During the seemingly interminable minute it took her, my grandfather stared out the window, at a spot somewhere between the sea and the mountains. When Louise had finished,

Dellamonica turned to Désiré and asked him to confirm what his mother had described. My uncle simply nodded. Louise then tendered a letter from the family doctor. This confirmed everything that had just been said. The specialist scanned the letter before quickly explaining what was known about the disease.

If one of Désiré's friends was infected with the AIDS virus, and they had shared needles, then yes, it was possible Désiré was also infected. As things stood, it was difficult to determine what percentage of those infected would go on to develop the disease. There was still hope that some would remain 'healthy carriers'. Dellamonica invited my uncle to go with him into a little recess at the back of his surgery. He listened to Désiré's breathing, examined his skin and the lining of his mouth, and felt his lymph nodes. He silently took notes throughout the examination. He gave Désiré a referral for a blood test and scheduled a follow-up appointment for the next month. Then he politely said goodbye to my grandfather and to my grandmother, who was exhausted after her confession.

Pierre Dellamonica did not even have the support of his own hospital. The head of the virology department had refused to analyse blood samples from his first patients for fear of infection. He proudly declared that he didn't work 'for queers and junkies'. Dellamonica had to make several trips to Paris to give the samples to Françoise Brun-Vézinet at Claude-Bernard, who carried out the tests in her laboratory and called him with the results a few weeks later.

Several floors down from Dellamonica's surgery, there were no other patients waiting to have blood taken. While my grandparents whispered impatiently to each other, Désiré watched as, behind the glass, the nurses passed his referral slip to each other before eventually leaving it on a pile of papers and disappearing. It was more than an hour before another nurse appeared. She looked very young. Perhaps she didn't have the self-assurance of her colleagues to flatly refuse to take a sample. As she scanned the piece of paper, she looked sadly at my uncle through the glass screen. Désiré assumed that she would simply put it back, but she called him in. After asking whether he had had to wait long, she drew some blood into a test tube while pretending not to see the track marks on his arm. She tried to seem friendly, though my uncle could see how careful she was being to keep as much distance as possible between them. Although he often elicited pity from those he met, this was the first time anyone had looked at him with such suspicion. A few minutes later, he was climbing into the back seat of his parents' car to head back to the village.

Some weeks after the tests, the verdict came: Désiré was seropositive. So was Brigitte, and so were most of their friends in the valley – or at least those who had agreed to take the test. They joined a long line of statistics that painted an increasingly alarming picture. According to initial estimates by health authorities, the region of Provence-Alpes-Côte d'Azur was among the worst affected in France, worse even than Île-de-France in terms of the number of people infected through drug use. In the hills and valleys in the hinterland of Nice, few villages were unscathed. Heroin had ensnared the young people of the villages, bringing the virus in its wake.

It was from the family doctor that my grandmother and my uncle found out that he was seropositive. This was confirmed at the second appointment with Professor Dellamonica. Désiré, who had been profoundly depressed since trying to quit heroin, simply sighed. His mother wanted to know as much as possible. Dellamonica explained that the LAV virus had been detected in her son's blood, but that did not mean that he actually had AIDS. Only when the virus began to attack the immune system would it be appropriate to talk about AIDS. At that point, her son would become ill. When my grandmother asked how long this might take, the doctor was equivocal. A few months, perhaps a few years, perhaps never. There was no way of knowing.

As soon as she walked out of the hospital, my grandmother once again retreated into herself, leaving everyone in the family with their own questions. Could the disease be cured? How was it transmitted? My mother read the few articles she could get her hands on. In the village, where the newsagent stocked only *Nice-Matin* and a handful of magazines, it was almost impossible to get information about the new virus.

On 15 July 1983, *Paris Match* ran the cover line 'The New Plague'. The article inside was very brief. Between pages of photos devoted to Joe Dassin's children and Sophie Marceau's holidays, the magazine published pictures of the dying Ken Ramsauer, a young American businessman hitherto unknown in France, who had insisted on bearing witness to his illness to the very end. On a double-page spread, two photos, taken only months apart, showed the ravages of AIDS on the body. They depicted the rise and fall of a young man. On the left, sexy and handsome; on the right, disfigured and barely recognizable. His puffy, swollen face exemplified the tragedy being played out on the other side of the Atlantic. Ken's partner Jim explained the first appearance of the symptoms, the gradual isolation, the family and friends who drifted away, the suffering, to say nothing of the condemnation by the medical community itself. 'The powerful words, the shocking photos' – the magazine didn't pull any punches, and concluded with a brief overview of the situation in France, from the first visit of the young airline steward to Claude-Bernard hospital two years earlier, through Jacques Leibowitch's work at Garches hospital that led to the virus being identified.

For my mother, it was like a slap in the face. Of the fifty-nine cases confirmed in France, she discovered, almost all involved homosexuals. The issue of heroin addicts was barely mentioned. She thumbed through the magazine over and over, rereading the article in search of some hope, some potential treatment, but in vain. There was no mention of promising research. She blew her cigarette smoke out the kitchen window. Then, to take her mind off things, she immersed herself in the celebrity pages of *Paris-Match*.

\*

My grandmother, for her part, pinned her hopes on the appointments she managed to get for her son with doctors at L'Archet. But these usually knowledgeable figures were suddenly taciturn. They spent more time observing than they did treating. They communicated though sighs and silence. Their only recommendation was that Désiré quit drugs for good. They admitted that they didn't know enough about the disease and were waiting on new information from Paris or the United States. They couldn't go beyond a diagnosis that sounded like a death sentence, and, for the time being, their advice was restricted to a few recommendations about everyday life: wash Désiré's cutlery separately with bleach; avoid sharp objects; keep Désiré away from anyone suffering from a disease, however treatable; in the event of injury, avoid all contact with Désiré's blood except while wearing latex gloves, then disinfect all surfaces again.

The smell of bleach. It is the one olfactory memory I have of my grandparents' house. The smell of Louise's despair, bringing her son home from hospital, the first plague victim in the village since the late Middle Ages. Even in a big hospital, even in a big city, there was nothing anyone could do for Désiré.

The asymptomatic phase of the illness became my grandmother's greatest ally. It offered a hiatus that made denial possible still. Symptoms of the disease among her son's friends would not be enough to persuade her to accept a reality that was now communal. On the contrary, she drew from it ever more arguments to set him apart from those doomed youths. All too often, those who dared speak the truth were faced with the full force of her fury, outbursts so violent that they brutally cut short any attempt at discussion. In the village, her son was not a junkie, he was not sick. He was just a little tired.

It was around this time that my grandfather disappeared. Émile was not dead, nor had he run away, he simply disappeared into some place in his thoughts. As Désiré's addiction and his illness became increasingly obvious to everyone, Émile poured all his energy and his commitment into his work, perhaps the only thing over which he still had any control. Louise was often absent, taking their son to medical appointments. He had to cover for her absence from the shop.

Trapped in his silence, he had no more energy to deal with the situation than his wife. Every afternoon, he would go out on his rounds, leaving the butcher's shop in the hands of his younger son and his daughter-in-law. Taking his truck, he escaped into the mountains, driving from hilltop village to deserted hamlet. It was here that he found refuge, on the roads he had travelled as a child with his father, buying cattle from local breeders, in the old farmhouses where he had learned his trade, in the houses inhabited by lonely women to whom he delivered perfume and cartons of cigarettes from the village. He would stay away until nightfall. He would spend Sunday afternoons washing the truck in the driveway, cleaning the butcher's knives, loading produce for the following day, all the while listening to the sports coverage on RMC radio. Never a howl. Never a tear. He remained unfathomable, a body and soul utterly engulfed by silence.

In time, Désiré's first symptoms would appear: the weight loss, the fever, the nausea, the diarrhoea, the coughing fits that wouldn't go away. It was these physical signs, far more than cell counts on a blood test, that would convince my grandmother of the gravity of the situation. So began an endless series of round trips, depending on my uncle's state of health. Shuttling between the village and the city, between his hospital room and his apartment, between using and withdrawal, between slow death and brief moments of reprieve. And between truth and denial. A doctor noting his patient's gradual decline. A mother who insists her son isn't suffering from a disease of homosexuals and junkies. A son who claims he is no longer using. Each to their own field: the doctor, science; the family, lies.

# T4

Towards the end of 1983, the epidemiologist Jean-Claude Gluckman and the immunologist David Klatzmann are tasked with describing how the virus discovered at Institut Pasteur attacks the immune system. Having observed a large number of patients at Pitié-Salpêtrière hospital, Klatzmann favours the theory that the virus attacks lymphocytes, since this would explain the total destruction of patients' immune systems. And it is true that the French team has observed a startling decrease of T4 lymphocytes in the blood taken from patients. This is something that has been noted in a number of American medical journals since 1981. Klatzmann agrees with many of his colleagues that the virus specifically targets these T4 lymphocytes, a family of white blood cells essential to the human body's natural defences.

Luc Montagnier finds this hypothesis persuasive and entrusts Klatzmann with providing scientific evidence to confirm the causal link between LAV and the onset of AIDS. This is a crucial task since there are still many scientists who suspect that the virus discovered at the Institut Pasteur is simply another opportunistic infection that affects patients who are severely immunocompromised. This would mean that LAV is merely another consequence of the disease.

Klatzmann's experiment is simple: he introduces the virus and T4 lymphocytes in the same cultures, then observes what happens in vitro. Having worked on transplant patients while in England, Klatzmann is familiar with a recently developed diagnostic tool known as lymphocyte typing: a single test that determines the various subgroups of lymphocytes in the immune system. In his laboratory at Pitié-Salpêtrière hospital, he isolates these subgroups of lymphocytes and cultures them. Half of the test tubes contain T4 cultures; the other half contain T8 lymphocytes. Placing the test tubes in an isothermal cooler, he takes them to Chermann's laboratory at Institut Pasteur, the only place equipped to culture the virus. Klatzmann sets himself up in the corner of the viral oncology unit dedicated to the study of LAV and places the virus in the presence of its T4 and T8 lymphocytes. Every day for a week, he visits the Institut Pasteur to observe any changes.

One Saturday morning, the Institut is almost deserted, since most of his colleagues are away for the weekend. Klatzmann bends over his microscope, studies the cultures and makes a crucial observation: the T4 lymphocytes exposed to the virus have been destroyed. These cultures have literally been wiped out, while those containing T8 lymphocytes are still intact. This initial experiment has confirmed Klatzmann's intuitions. He immediately informs his colleagues.

The experiment must be replicated many times in order

to remove any possible doubt, but Klatzmann is convinced that, for the first time in the world, he has just reproduced in a lab what has been happening in his patients' blood. A series of similar experiments is carried out, all of which produce the same result: LAV infects and destroys T4 lymphocytes. Klatzmann and Luc Montagnier quickly write up an article about this major discovery and send it to *Nature*.

Weeks pass, months pass. Still there is no response from the magazine. They begin to lose hope; no one seems interested in their discovery. Luc Montagnier picks up the phone to demand an explanation.

The editors at *Nature* are categorical: the article has been rejected. They cite reservations from the scientific committee about the reliability of David Klatzmann's results: his working methods and his results are questionable, too tenuous for a journal as prestigious as *Nature*. Luc Montagnier has another, more subjective explanation for this curious rejection: *Nature* is determined not to upset researchers in the US. The magazine wants to give them time to catch up with their French counterparts.

The article headlined 'T-lymphocyte T4 Molecule Behaves as the Receptor for Human Retrovirus LAV' is finally published in *Nature* a year later, in the issue dated 20 December 1984.

# MONEY

My mother's parents had also been born in the village, but hailed from more modest stock. After the pasta factory closed, my maternal grandfather worked as a driver for a small construction company while his wife worked on her brother's farm. Fields of vegetables stretching as far as the eye could see along the old riverbed. But, in the end, hailstones, insects and drought would strike and they never harvested as much as they hoped. After many years spent toiling, they had been able to afford what was known as 'land'. A small plot outside the village on which my grandfather would spend years building a house that only became habitable as they were nearing retirement. There, they had a vegetable garden, they kept hens and rabbits, more out of necessity than to pass the time.

One afternoon, as my grandfather was tending the garden and my grandmother, sitting on a bench made from a railway sleeper, was topping and tailing beans, a strange vehicle drove up the lane leading to their house. The yellow BMW pulled up outside. My mother's parents recognized their daughter's brother- and sister-in-law. Désiré and Brigitte greeted them and explained that they were visiting friends and family, asking for money to help finance a project dear to their hearts: they wanted to build a house.

My grandparents were accustomed to greeting the tramps who roam the byways of France, stopping at houses to beg for a few provisions before continuing on their way. They said apologetically that all they could afford was the money they had set aside for the Sunday shopping. When my grandmother offered to give them some eggs and vegetables from their garden, the couple politely refused.

Their diagnosis had done nothing to change their drugs habit. They drove the length and breadth of the valley, calling on friends, cousins, friends of friends and cousins of cousins, always coming up with some new excuse for why they needed to borrow money they would never repay. They offered endless explanations: they needed a new car, to buy a gift, to pay for medicine, to get ready for the birth of their child . . . Brigitte was pregnant. They had only just found out. It had happened shortly after they were first diagnosed, and the doctors were very circumspect, but Désiré and Brigitte clung to this pregnancy as proof of a future.

Within the family, we had been told never to give them a centime. We knew they were still taking drugs. For a long time, the till in the butcher's shop had provided an inexhaustible supply of cash. But the village was no longer the prosperous little place where the family had made its reputation. Customers were fewer and less wealthy now, and my grandparents were no longer in the first flush of youth.

Whenever Désiré and Brigitte managed to scrounge some money, the BMW would be seen hurtling through the valley, with Désiré behind the wheel, wearing yellow tinted sunglasses, flooring the accelerator, and Brigitte pale and shivering in the passenger seat. They always went to the same place, a cafe in one of the eastern districts of Nice. There, in the back room, far from the music, the public bar, the staring eyes, they would talk about drugs and nothing else. The drug you need, the drug that brings relief, the drug that costs, the drug that warms, the drug that ... everything. Heroin. Heroin and then nothingness. Heroin and then death. The deal would be quickly done. They no longer haggled over the price.

As soon as they had gear in their pockets, they'd get back into the BMW and park a few hundred metres away, in a deserted suburban street. As soon as the needle went in, they would slump in their seats, asleep, free from pain and craving for a few hours.

For some time now, pain had displaced pleasure. After several weeks spent getting wasted, not long after they first met, Désiré and Brigitte went cold turkey for a few days. Then they woke up one morning tired, feverish and aching all over. Strictly speaking, they were not sick. Heroin was calling to them. This was the first time they felt they were dependent. A feeling that never left them. So began the endless fall. Now that they couldn't work, they couldn't earn money. They were no longer seeking pleasure, or bliss, or the sort of transcendental experience Désiré first discovered one night at a party in Amsterdam. The vice-like grip felt unbreakable. Désiré and Brigitte even stopped eating. Their fingers no longer felt a thrill when they touched. Heroin had taken everything: their appetite, their sleep, their lovemaking. It compelled them to try to recapture an inner, unreachable pleasure. Life had become a senseless race against the symptoms of withdrawal, a race lost before it had begun.

Their very existence was redefined, reappraised: it now had a precise value. A hundred francs. That was roughly the cost of a baggie of cheap smack in Nice, a banknote filched from the till at the butcher's shop, a lie to a friend, a couple of car radios, a handful of records from Désiré's collection . . . My uncle's apartment grew bigger from the empty spaces left by addiction. Records, furniture, clothes, ornaments . . . anything and everything that could be sold.

Cough syrup, aspirin and painkillers began to disappear from the family medicine cabinet. In an effort to get off heroin, Désiré and Brigitte sought solace in other drugs. A number of common household medicines contained codeine, an opiate, like heroin, extracted from the poppy. It alleviated the symptoms of withdrawal a little. But all their attempts to get clean had ended in failure.

Drugs were an uncharted ocean on which my uncle Désiré and Brigitte drifted. Their family and friends had all had medicines, jewellery and money stolen from them. My father could not understand how someone could steal from those closest to him. In a family where love was not professed, affection was expressed through food and money. The money that was given, lent or donated, and the money that was denied. The meals that my grandmother made, and the cuts of meat my grandfather set aside in the cold room for their dinners with their children, were the proof of a love that was reciprocated, an expression of silent feelings. Whenever my grandmother noticed that there was money missing from the till, my father would merely sigh in patois: 'Sabès' (You know).

One day, Brigitte and Désiré told the family that they had decided to get married. Louise was thrilled; this was wonderful news, it offered hope that they were back on the straight and narrow. My father wasn't fooled for a second. His brother had never talked about wanting to marry. He simply knew that the prospect of a wedding would make the family more generous.

Looking at them again today, I realize just how much the footage my father filmed on that grey morning outside the chapel of the monastery in Cimiez was staged. I study every detail, peer at the blurry faces on the film. Something does not add up. Brigitte's very simple dress, the way that she and Désiré exchange a few private words, the stiffness of the whole family. In my father's collection of Super-8 reels, there are at least a dozen weddings. This one is like no other. There are very few guests, no friends, only immediate family. The whole thing is small, subdued, hurriedly organized.

And now Désiré and Brigitte were expecting a baby. My father, who had just had twins, worried for the future of this child who would be born into such tragic circumstances, where drugs or disease were destined to take her parents' lives. Others in the family, like Louise, chose to see this pregnancy as a glimmer of hope. She believed the new baby would finally force Désiré and Brigitte to quit heroin and look after themselves. But her younger son no longer believed in redemption. He knew exactly how it would all end. As Désiré's blood slowly curdled, a mute rage was born in my father's veins, one that would never leave him.

# ELISA

In February 1983, although the connection between the LAV virus and the onset of AIDS is yet to be proven, discussions are held every Saturday at the Institut Pasteur about developing a screening test. Currently, the only tool at Luc Montagnier's disposal is radioimmunoprecipitation assay (RIPA), a cumbersome, time-consuming and expensive test, ill-suited to the urgency of the situation. During the initial meetings, they decide to develop a more efficient method. While researchers at the Institut continue to observe the virus in patients, at Claude-Bernard hospital, Françoise Brun-Vézinet, the director of virology, and her student Christine Rouzioux start working to develop a test. They are interested in a recent innovation in serology known as enzyme-linked immunosorbent assay or ELISA, a chemical test that detects the presence of an antigen through antibodies in a blood sample. It is a technique that Françoise Brun-Vézinet has already adapted to detect cytomegalovirus, a virus belonging to the herpes family. She plans to do the same with LAV. But in order to identify antibodies specific to LAV, she needs antigens specific to the virus. Claude-Bernard hospital does not have sufficient resources to cultivate these antigens. Her relationship with the Institut Pasteur will prove critical.

On 13 July 1983, Luc Montagnier sends an initial batch of antigens to Claude-Bernard hospital. There they are studied by Françoise Brun-Vézinet and Christine Rouzioux, who learn to recognize the antibodies present and develop an initial series of tests. Within a week, they have succeeded in producing preliminary results that are encouraging. By 20 July, tests on blood samples from infected patients are producing good results, but in percentages that are still too low. In September, as they continue to hone their methods, 30 to 40 per cent of samples taken from patients elicit positive results. Meanwhile, blood samples taken from people known to be completely healthy are also generating positive results. The virologists, however, are not discouraged by the fact that the percentage of 'true positives' is too low and that there are still a large number of 'false positives'.

In France, the number of patients identified is still very low compared with the hundreds of cases reported in the United States, meaning that Françoise Brun-Vézinet and her student do not have sufficient material to work with. So they appeal to the CDC in Atlanta, which agrees to send large quantities of infected blood samples.

In the spring of 1984, an article published in *The Lancet* details the results of a French study carried out on more than 500 infected patients. The study has made it possible to detect LAV-specific antibodies in the blood samples of these patients. Although in time the retrovirus will completely destroy the immune system, the antibodies do not give up without a fight. It is through these ineffective antibodies that the body reveals the presence of the virus.

It will be months before the ELISA procedure adapted to the AIDS virus is sensitive enough to constitute an acceptable screening tool. By the end of 1984, the process jointly developed by Claude-Bernard hospital and the Institut Pasteur is able to detect LAV-specific antibodies in 90 per cent of cases, with no false positives. Christine Rouzioux's long months spent working alongside Françoise Brun-Vézinet will be the subject of her final-year thesis in virology.

The functional French test, patented by the Institut Pasteur, and its American rival, developed by Abbott Laboratories, will not be available to the general public until the summer of 1985.

# TREATMENTS

It all began with a long overdue phone call. The village doctor called to say that Désiré would soon be offered a place in a drug rehabilitation centre. Since the centre was much in demand, the family had to persuade my uncle not to miss his appointment.

Louise helped her son pack his case. She ironed his clothes and drove him to Nice. With Désiré admitted to the glass-and-steel annex of the hospital, and before any symptoms of the disease had appeared, hope seemed possible again.

Treatment began with a one-to-one interview with a toxicologist. As the doctor read my uncle's file, he gave no reaction beyond a series of sighs. When he had finished, he explained the process of the three to four week stay. Désiré would have to read and sign the rules of the clinic. In addition to agreeing not to leave the clinic or to receive any visitors, Désiré had to attend a series of group therapy sessions and individual appointments with a psychologist.

During his first detox, Désiré drew a kind of diagram representing a circle. Addiction was a response to frustration, a lack of self-confidence, a fissure that the drug helped alleviate. It was a vicious circle. The fissure was filled by heroin, which led to nothing except more heroin. The doctor explained to Désiré that he would be able to quit heroin only when he identified and closed this fissure.

My uncle had grown up in a family where people didn't talk to each other. I wonder whether he even attempted to share his deepest feelings with a stranger. I picture him nodding silently to get this over with as quickly as possible. I will never know whether, during these sessions, he learned anything about himself.

Quitting had to be total, not gradual. As a result, the first week was the most gruelling. Désiré struggled with nausea, aches and pains, and blinding headaches. The physical symptoms of withdrawal. Substitution treatments such as methadone were not yet licensed in France and would not be until 1995, when the government finally acknowledged the ravages of the AIDS epidemic among addicts. Consequently, nurses could only prescribe him painkillers and antispasmodics, and occasionally sedatives or tranquillizers, but only when the withdrawal symptoms were most severe. In the clinic, as in hospital, many of the nursing staff were terrified by Désiré's illness, all the more so since the difficulties of withdrawal led to a tense atmosphere.

Once he had got through the first few days, Désiré felt better. His relationship with the staff was more relaxed. He would start on an intense phase of psychological work. This was all the more necessary since the symptoms of withdrawal now manifested themselves as anxiety, confusion and depression.

From the window of his bedroom, between the hills of

Nice, he could just glimpse the sea and the far horizon. In order to get through this, he probably spent his time thinking about Brigitte and their unborn baby.

For the family, each treatment was a period of hope and relief. Hope that this time would be the last. Relief that they no longer had to worry about where Désiré might be. He would leave the village for weeks at a time, and his parents' worry was eased somewhat. No one knew what he did or what was done to him in that place, but they were relieved that they did not have to worry about getting a call from the ambulance service or from some villager who had found Désiré unconscious, with a needle in his arm. My grandmother would go back to her job behind the butcher's counter and relieve my father and grandfather of the tiredness accumulated during her absences.

In this place that looked like a hospital but did not use the term, Désiré tried to keep himself busy. When he was allowed to use the phone, he would call to say that things were going well, that everything would be fine now. The scars on his arms were healing. His complexion had improved. He looked human again. My grandmother was already picturing him back behind a desk at the solicitor's office.

My uncle did his best to take an interest in something other than drugs, but he did not know how. He had completely forgotten how he used to spend his time before heroin. And since he could not find an answer, everyone in the family tried to remind him. Now that Désiré was far from the temptations of the streets and of his friends, they played for time. If they could not win the battle, they might at least win a truce. For a while, they could postpone defeat.

# THE TEST

In 1984, Jacques Leibowitch at Raymond-Poincaré hospital in Garches becomes aware of the risk that the virus is being spread through blood transfusions. It is a concern shared by his colleagues in America and those at the Institut Pasteur, who are seeing an increasing number of AIDS patients who are neither gay nor drug addicts, all of whom have received blood transfusions.

In France, and in the United States, an urgent alert goes out about the need to test blood bags destined for use in transfusions. But screening techniques are still in short supply, and the patients who need blood cannot wait. Like his colleagues at the Institut Pasteur and in the USA, Jacques Leibowitch is working hard to develop a simple, rapid test that can be used in blood banks to detect the presence of the virus.

In his laboratory, he and his colleague Dominique Mathez, who has provided him with a small portable incubator, work tirelessly until, finally, they manage to get satisfactory results using a tried and tested technique known as immunofluorescence. This traditional method is very time-consuming. Dominique Mathez and her colleagues have to culture the blood samples for forty-eight to seventy-two hours before they can detect the presence of the virus.

Also in 1984, Leibowitch continues to visit Robert Gallo's teams in the USA. He shares the latest discoveries with an ever-growing audience and gives numerous talks to colleagues in France. On his return from a visit to the United States, Leibowitch gives a lecture at Tarnier hospital. Among the audience are the doctors who have been trying for several months to treat the philosopher Michel Foucault.

Foucault first consulted them because he was suffering from a persistent cough. The fact that he is gay is an open secret, so the possibility that this may be AIDS crosses their minds, but the doctors are initially reluctant to stop there, determined not to be swayed by clichéd preconceptions about the disease. Having been successfully treated with a course of antibiotics, in the spring of 1984 Foucault suffers a sudden relapse that forces his doctors to question their initial diagnosis. What they learn from Jacques Leibowitch confirms their initial fears.

Kaposi's sarcoma remains widely associated with AIDS, and the condition is still considered to be a *sine qua non* for making the diagnosis. Even Foucault, who has regularly visited New York where AIDS is wreaking havoc, has been swayed by this idea. Since he is not suffering from KS, those around him are reassuring. Moreover, the philosopher wants to carry on working for as long as possible, and his close friends feel that such a diagnosis would be crushing. As a result, in the weeks that follow, they maintain a code of silence.

When, finally, he has to be admitted, Foucault's doctors do not send him to Willy Rozenbaum's ward at Pitié-Salpêtrière hospital, so as not to fuel media speculation. Until the very end, he will be told nothing about his true illness. When the philosopher dies in June 1984, his partner Daniel Defert is shocked to see four letters on the death certificate stating the cause of death: AIDS. Outraged, Defert sets up AIDES, an association dedicated to helping those suffering from the virus.

At Garches hospital, Jacques Leibowitch and Dominique Mathez make significant advances on their screening test between 10 October and 12 December 1984. In an initial trial on 10,000 blood samples, there were only one or two false positives. Using this process, they test samples taken from blood bags from all over Île-de-France in order to estimate the percentage of infected batches in the region's blood banks. The results are terrifying. Out of 2,000 blood bags tested, they found twenty infected. Meanwhile, researchers at the Institut Pasteur have proved that patients receiving blood from infected donors have themselves become seropositive. Haemophiliacs, who regularly receive blood concentrates from a large number of donors, are particularly at risk. Leibowitch tries to raise the alarm at the Ministry of Health, but with little success, since his headstrong approach tends to rile almost everyone he talks to.

During this period, the Institut Pasteur has developed a technique that uses heat to virally inactivate blood products, neutralizing the virus in blood bags without affecting the quality of the blood. But, like their mule-headed colleague in Garches, the researchers at the Institut cannot persuade the ministry to take their warnings seriously.

The authorities appear to be betting on the hypothesis that not all those who test positive will go on to develop AIDS. It is a deadly gamble. Their negligence and their desire to save money will result in thousands of people becoming infected.

# BIRTH

In the spring of 1984, Brigitte gave birth to a baby girl. In keeping with family tradition, she was named in honour of Émile, her paternal grandfather. Like Désiré, Émilie inherited the name of her father's father. In becoming a father himself, my uncle found the new lease of life that his ailing body denied him. From the drugs that had robbed them of everything, he and Brigitte had managed to wrest a child.

My grandmother was all the more thrilled since she had only two grandchildren, both boys. Her granddaughter was a symbol of the hope that Désiré and Brigitte would finally put heroin behind them.

From the outset, the doctors at L'Archet had been clear: the virus responsible for AIDS had been detected in children born to infected parents. They had already recorded a number of infected newborn babies at the hospital.

While they had made no attempt to influence the couple's decision, they had warned Désiré and Brigitte not only that was there a chance their child would be born seropositive, but that their own limited life expectancy meant they were unlikely to see her grow up. When Émilie was born, doctors detected LAV-specific antibodies in her blood. It was possible that these were antibodies passed on by her mother. Only after several weeks could they come to a definite conclusion.

I've often tried to imagine the confused mixture of feelings Émilie's arrival must have elicited in the family: a mixture of genuine happiness and terrible fear. Would she inherit her parents' virus? Would she develop the disease? How could they possibly know, when even the doctors could not answer these questions with any certainty?

Today, I find it very difficult to imagine my father as anything other than anguished by Émilie's birth. He could not celebrate the birth of his first niece without worrying about her future. As though, from the first, he was aware of the thwarted destiny of this new life. Human beings are not meant to witness the death of a child they have seen born. Perhaps he had understood. We were doomed. Doomed to outlive Émilie, doomed to outlive the three of them. Such a thought would have been all the more unbearable for my father, who had learned to keep his feelings to himself. He had never told anyone about his brother's addiction, his illness, his decision to have a child. He was unlikely to start now. As for my mother, she scoured newspapers, TV programmes and the few books on the subject to try to understand. She wanted to find some reason to hope.

When they left the maternity ward, the young parents took their baby home to the rooftop apartment above the cafe on the place de la Fontaine. Villagers congratulated the couple when they saw them push the navy-blue pram along the school road. They looked beautiful and happy. The days of wild parties, drugs and all-nighters seemed far behind them. My grandmother popped in several times a day to help. Mostly, she wanted to check that they had not gone back to their old ways. She would come up with spurious reasons to open kitchen cupboards, the drawers of nightstands, the medicine cabinet, to surreptitiously check for drugs, rubber bands or needles, and more often than not, she went away reassured.

Given the results of her blood tests, Émilie was closely monitored by the village doctor, the infectious disease specialists at L'Archet and those at Lenval, the paediatric hospital in Nice. Within her first few weeks, additional tests confirmed that the virus was indeed there, under her skin, coursing through the veins of a little girl who looked no different from any other, a dormant virus that might one day wake up.

# AZT

In the spring of 1984, Robert Gallo gives a sample of LAV to Hiroaki Mitsuya, a virologist at the National Cancer Institute. He is keen to have the institute's researchers test every molecule of the sample, in the hope that one of them may be able to prevent the virus from replicating. To increase their chances of success, the institute calls on a number of other laboratories, including Burroughs Wellcome in North Carolina. Virology is not particularly profitable, so Burroughs Wellcome, which believes that it has potential, is one of the few laboratories specializing in this field.

After several weeks, the researchers at Burroughs Wellcome turn their attention to BW509U, a compound synthesized by Dr Jerome Horwitz in 1964, somewhere in Michigan. Horwitz had used the synthetic compound in his experiments on certain cancers caused by viruses. BW509U was quickly abandoned, in part because of the debilitating side effects in patients, but mostly because it proved ineffective. Horowitz and his colleagues had synthesized a number of other compounds at the time, including ddC, d4T and ddI, but all had proved ineffective against cancer. The researchers at Burroughs Wellcome come upon the compound while searching through the archives of their chemical library. Initially, they carry out tests on mice inoculated with a retrovirus. After a number of assays, they notice that BW509U inhibits virus replication in the mice. Despite the fact that tests carried out at other laboratories seem to show that the compound is ineffective, Burroughs Wellcome sends a sample, renamed 'compound S', to the National Cancer Institute. Here, Hiroaki Mitsuya can carry out a more detailed study of the compound, not on mice, but on the samples of the human virus given to him by Robert Gallo. He cultures the virus with clones of T4 lymphocytes taken from his own blood. By the end of 1984, the work bears out his hope that it will have a significant effect: the compound, now renamed azidothymidine or AZT, inhibits replication of the AIDS virus in vitro and blocks its action on lymphocytes. It is time to organize clinical trials in human beings.

In July 1985, an initial study on nineteen patients concludes that AZT tends to increase their T4 cell count. Trials are subsequently carried out on larger numbers of patients.

In June 1986, a double-blind study charts the progress of the disease in 282 patients. Half are given AZT, the other half are given a placebo. In September, after just eight weeks of treatment, the results are significant: there has been only one death in the group treated with AZT, compared to nineteen in those given the placebo. Moreover, twenty-four patients in the AZT group developed full-blown AIDS, compared with forty-five in those receiving the placebo. At least in the short term, it seems that people are less likely to die when given AZT.

For the first time in years, a drug has demonstrated a degree of effectiveness in the fight against AIDS. Although it does not actually kill the virus, it seems to be able to halt its destructive logic. In the face of the growing epidemic, the Food and Drug Administration fast-track their review of AZT and approve it in March 1987.

In 1989, ACTG protocol 019, involving more than 3,000 patients, is prematurely terminated. The difference in rates of mortality and of developing full-blown AIDS between those treated with AZT and those given placebos is so great it has raised ethical concerns: why continue to administer a placebo if AZT seems so effective? Burroughs Wellcome proudly announces its results. The day after these are published by the American press, the company's shares jump 32 per cent in the space of a few hours.

# THE HOSPITAL

'I'm the one in charge of the needles here, got that?'

Désiré got it. It was in his best interests to get well and get the hell out as quickly as possible. No sooner had he settled into the hospital room than a nurse built like a brick shithouse showed up and tried to scare him with this comment. The guy moved between the bed and the window, as if in conquered territory. Then he vanished.

The hospital staff were terrified of drug addicts. When they were in withdrawal, they were capable of anything. They would steal syringes and drugs from the trolleys, they would fly into violent rages. Sometimes, visiting friends would covertly slip them drugs and they would be found unconscious in their room or in the bathroom. Why bother treating people so intent on killing themselves?

With the AIDS epidemic, more and more drug addicts had been admitted to the pneumology department of Pasteur hospital in Nice. They came to be treated for the tuberculosis and the pneumocystosis caught because of a virus they contracted while sharing needles. From the outset, the staff kept a watchful eye on them. Addicts were required to sign up to a code of conduct, and stringent efforts were made to bring them to heel. They were the ones who should be made to feel fear.

Désiré's first stretch in hospital, aside from the detox treatments, was for tuberculosis. For more than a month, he had been suffering from a persistent cough and shortness of breath that left him exhausted. When he began coughing up blood, his mother took him to Nice. His stay lasted a few weeks; as soon as the antibiotics had taken effect, he went back to the village. This first illness took its toll on the pale, gaunt body weakened by years of using heroin. Brigitte was doing her best to take care of Émilie, so it was Louise who sat by her son's bedside. She recognized his room in the hospital maze by the red sticker on the door. What, at first, she mistook for special consideration was in fact only the first of a never-ending series of humiliations. Louise often arrived in the early afternoon to find her son's lunch tray left outside his door. Désiré was always the last to be treated, if the nurses didn't forget him altogether. One day, Louise found Désiré caked in dried blood. None of the carers had come to clean him up after a haemorrhage. My grandmother was about to throw a fit when my uncle intervened. 'Don't, Maman, it's fine. We'll manage.' Louise was beginning to understand. She cleaned up her son's blood. The same blood that terrified the hospital staff, the lifeblood she had given him, the blood that was slowly killing him. She spent long hours with Désiré. She would help him up and walk him up and down the corridors, bring cold cuts from the butcher's shop and fruit from the greengrocer. And she would prattle on about anything that took him away from this hospital room: Brigitte and Émilie, the building work on her brother's house, the butcher's shop, the latest village gossip. Perhaps in these intimate moments, they were finally able to talk to each other. I can imagine her questioning him, trying to understand what he got out of drugs. Why couldn't he quit after all the destruction drugs had caused? He was a parent now, she would remind him through her tears, his daughter needed a father, a father who could still stand.

During the last part of his convalescence, Désiré shared his room with a young man who had almost no visitors. Except for another man who would sit for hours, holding his hand and kissing him. It was the first time Louise had witnessed such a scene. If she was a little embarrassed at first, she ended up smiling, thanks to a few knowing winks from Désiré, and because she was moved to discover that this was love. A love as genuine as her love for her son.

Her only impression of homosexuality dated back to her childhood in Italian Piedmont. A memory of howls, of blows, of spitting. She had seen two men being beaten because they had been caught in a barn together. The village boys had proudly dragged them to the main square, yelling to attract the other villagers. Lured by this unusual commotion, Louise had run outside with her brothers and sisters. When the mob began to brutally beat their prey, the terrified little girl pressed her face into her mother's skirts. It was one of her last memories from before the war.

Out in the hospital corridor, alone with Désiré, my grandmother said: 'But apart from his friend, is there no one else who comes to see that young man?'

It was on this pneumology ward set aside for the first AIDS patients that Louise finally came to understand the illness that was eating away at her son. Doctor Dellamonica had warned her. After the tuberculosis, he was likely to contract other diseases in the weeks or months ahead. Surrounded by his companions in misery, most of them gay men or drug addicts, she could no longer deny the obvious. The virus was dragging her back to all the things she had fought so hard to escape. It had frustrated the plan she had followed ever since she left Italy. This pathogen that had come from nowhere, had put an end to her long history of upward mobility, her struggle to be respected, to be someone. It rekindled the feelings of shame, rejection and humiliation that she had long since vowed never to feel again.

Only this disease had made it possible for a mother to see her son as others saw him: a junkie rotting among his own kind. An addict doomed to the same fate as his friends. Here, nothing mattered, not his name, not the hopes his parents had nurtured for him, not the standing of his family. AIDS did not care about anything. It made fools of everyone: researchers, doctors, patients and their families. No one escaped, not even the favourite son of a family of shopkeepers from a valley in the *arrière-pays*.

# HPA-23

At the Institut Pasteur, as the researchers from the laboratories leave for the night, they occasionally find a young man or a young woman waiting outside, clutching a sheet of paper. The face, the gauntness, the despair in the eyes and, in some cases, the broken French tinged with an American twang say all there is to say. The scientists understand immediately.

Since the spring of 1983, some time before interest became focused on AZT, Jean-Claude Chermann has been testing Heteropolyanion 23 or HPA-23, a viral inhibitor designed to stop LAV replication. This is the world's first antiretroviral drug. Chermann first discovered it in 1972. It appears to temporarily inhibit the virus, tending to slow the process responsible for the disease. Initial results have been encouraging, despite the fact that the side effects of HPA-23 are toxic to certain blood cells.

From New York to San Francisco, word has spread that researchers at the Institut Pasteur are trialling a drug that may block the action of the virus in the blood. On the advice of doctors who can do nothing more for them, desperate young people are leaving their towns, their country to come to Paris. Utterly exhausted, they ask only to take part in one of the Institut's trials.

Medical researchers have rarely come so close to death or been so brutally confronted by their own failures. Usually, that fate is reserved for doctors. The AIDS epidemic has turned everything on its head, particularly the relationship between researcher and patient. It has made communication between the two groups essential, and broken down the barriers that have long separated them. Suddenly, failures of research can be seen not only on statistical reports and computer screens, but on these desperate faces.

The researchers are much the same age as these young patients; they know they are utterly alone, that they have been abandoned by those closest to them. What sets them apart? Their sexual orientation? Their drug use? What justifies the support and respect for the researcher and the contempt for the dying patient? Granted, the teams at the Institut Pasteur are at the forefront of global AIDS research, but what satisfaction can there be in that so long as people are coming to die in their arms? These are ghosts that will haunt them for years to come.

One night, while tending to a patient in palliative care, Françoise Barré-Sinoussi hears a faint voice through an oxygen mask, struggling to be heard above the noise of the respirator: 'Thank you.' The young woman is confused: 'Why? We haven't been able to save you.' His eyes half-closed, caught between two worlds, the dying man still finds the strength to say: 'It's not for me. It's for the others.'

# UNDER THE TONGUE

Already, it is a scene that exists only in black and white. Or at least that is how I see it, because there is no colour in the photographs. It comes alive thanks to the movies that were made back then; it is from these that my brain found something that could animate it.

Two schoolkids are walking down the rue du 4-Septembre. Two boys in their early teens. The elder walks in front, the younger follows close behind, carrying his brother's schoolbag in his arms, and his own on his back. Like every other morning, they stop by the butcher's shop before heading to school. While the younger boy hugs his father, the older creeps into the back of the shop and takes two of the large rubber bands used to secure the rolls of wrapping paper. Then I see them leave the shop and carry on their way.

At the corner of the street, the brothers do not cross the bridge. They turn right and disappear. Down the dirt tracks that run along the riverbank, through the groves of oak to the limestone hills that tower over the village, escaping the hoarfrost that blankets the valley. In a tumbledown sheepfold that belongs to their grandfather, they set to work making catapults, build a hut and play Cowboys and Indians. A few days ago, they had had to get their mother to sign a form sent home by the teacher, authorizing the school nurse to vaccinate them.

To avoid the sting of the terrifying needle, Désiré and my father treated themselves to a day spent bunking off. They would go home at the usual time. The only evidence of their transgression would be revealed in the absence of a stamp on their Child Health Records. Engrossed in their work, their parents would not notice. Some months later, the family doctor would be puzzled to discover a blank space in the list of compulsory vaccinations.

Twenty years later, if Désiré were to disappear for even a moment, my grandmother would panic, terrified that he might relapse. Her son had promised he would stop taking drugs. The scars on his arms were healing. She searched his apartment several times and found no drugs in any room or cupboard. In a world where there was no cure for AIDS, at least she could hope that he was cured of heroin. To Louise, withdrawal was something tangible, more concrete than a retrovirus. She still hoped that the disease would eventually leave the body that the drug had allowed it to infect. That her son would go back to his brilliant career and finally be a credit to the family name she had worked so hard to wash clean of village gossip, of the pitying looks of paramedics, of the shame and the needles.

The doctors, however, told her point-blank: not only

was the disease advancing, but Désiré was still taking drugs. More and more, in fact.

Eventually, my uncle confessed that he had never given up. Despite the stints in rehab, and attempts to withdraw using cannabis, codeine and anything he could get his hands on, he had been unable to break the grip of heroin. He had simply found a more inconspicuous way of using, injecting into a vein under the tongue, where no one would think to check. It was this chilling revelation that finally made his parents realize that they had lost the battle.

# ROCK HUDSON

On Thursday, 25 July 1985, Rock Hudson is rushed to the American Hospital in Neuilly after collapsing in his room at the Ritz. Rumours spread so quickly that his press officer is forced to issue a statement: the legendary Hollywood actor has AIDS. He was diagnosed in the United States a year ago. The star, whose fans only now discover that he is homosexual, had come to Paris in a last hope of being treated. Having run out of options, his doctors in the USA told him about an experimental protocol in France. For Hudson, as for so many others, being part of the trials for the antiretroviral drug HPA-23 offered a last glimmer in a sky in which no stars now shone.

On the day he collapsed at the Ritz, he had been expected to go to another hospital to continue with his treatment. As soon as he came round at the American Hospital in Neuilly, he told the nursing staff that he was seropositive. His admission did not remain a secret for long.

Within hours, in a wave of panic, the wards of the American Hospital and the maternity unit are emptied. The board of the celebrated hospital ask the patient to leave the premises as soon as possible. Faced with a media storm, Rock Hudson decides to go back to the United States. No airline will allow him to board a plane. The actor is forced to personally charter a Boeing 747 to get back to California. By the time he arrives, the American media is already broadcasting news of his illness on an endless loop. Reporters loudly wonder whether he may have infected other stars of his era during on-screen kisses.

Rock Hudson is one of the first popular stars to go public about his illness. In the eyes of the world, AIDS has finally got a face, the face of a fallen star.

The actor will die a few weeks later in his Beverly Hills home.

As for the HPA-23 trials in France, they will soon be abandoned because the results are unsatisfactory.

# THE OTHERS

A few months after his painful convalescence from tuberculosis, Désiré contracted pneumocystis pneumonia, forcing him to leave the village again. In hospital, the infections multiplied. He developed oesophageal candidiasis and caught infections from mycobacteria. His beleaguered immune system was simply unable to fight them off.

Once again, my grandmother visited as often as possible, helplessly watching the harrowing spectacle of her son fading away. Little by little, his pale, gaunt body sank deeper into the white sheets of his bed.

Gone. Gone was the carefree party boy known throughout the valley for his nocturnal escapades. His bronzed skin had turned ashen and his body, once draped in flashy, fashionable clothes, was reduced to skin and bone. His happy-go-lucky spirit, his lust for life, all the things that once set him apart in a stolid family, devoted to work, were disappearing along with his immune system. It might soon be time to say goodbye. I find it hard to believe that anyone in the family would have dared broach the subject. My grandmother, too busy hoping that sooner or later the impossible would happen, talked to him about hanging on, for his daughter, for his wife, for them, for himself, until a cure could be found.

On this occasion, Désiré was on a multidisciplinary ward specially dedicated to patients with AIDS. The abuse he had experienced on other wards was less frequent there – though some of the staff still made distinctions between patients. Addicts got less compassion when they frustrated the efforts of staff to get them back on their feet. Staff were also disconcerted by seropositive women who had decided to become pregnant despite the known risks. Even in a department dedicated to patients suffering from it, AIDS remained a curious illness, circumscribed as it was by moral judgements, by notions of good and evil forever linked to the concept of sin. The private sins of having explored their sexuality, had homosexual sex, injected heroin, hidden the fact that they were seropositive from partners or people with whom they shared needles, and of wanting to have a child they knew was likely to die. Some patients were more guilty than others.

The good and the bad, the innocent victims and the guilty – the conversations that swirled around AIDS impinged on our family and divided it. My grandmother painted a portrait of three victims doomed by fate: her son, her daughter-in-law and her granddaughter. My grandfather retreated into silence. He felt suffocated by the labels and the stereotypes associated with the disease. Raising the subject would mean discussing things for which he had no vocabulary, topics he didn't have the courage to broach. He fled this oppressive atmosphere for the safety of the butcher's shop. It hardly mattered that the villages he toured in his truck were mostly deserted now; work was his way of escape. As for my father, in his unspoken anger, I think he drew a clear distinction between the little girl he thought of as a victim and her parents whom he considered guilty. Guilty of imposing their early death on her, and guilty of leaving their rancid blood as her inheritance.

The government was slow to recognize the tragedy unfolding beneath the fluorescent lights of hospital wards, leaving patients and their families utterly distraught. They had to wait until the second half of the 1980s – an eternity, given the urgency of the pandemic – before the Ministry of Social Affairs authorized advertisements for condoms, and launched free anonymous screening centres. The first ad on television didn't even mention how the virus was transmitted. In 1986, Michèle Barzach, Minister for Health in the government led by Jacques Chirac, received a steady stream of reports on the vast number of infections among intravenous drug users. The reports emphasized high-risk practices, and showed that needles were sometimes shared by dozens of people. This alarming discovery led to the 1987 law liberalizing the sale of syringes. The following year, Human Immunodeficiency Care and Information Centres (CISIH) were set up in hospitals. Their goal was to coordinate comprehensive medical, psychological and social care for patients within dedicated departments. Small units with specially trained staff would be set up.

At L'Archet hospital, despite the relentless increase of

new AIDS patients and the constant deaths, the staff were as humane as possible. Many of the orderlies, nurses and doctors had ended up here by chance, while finishing their studies. Others chose to work here out of personal conviction, sometimes after the loss of a loved one they wished they could have helped. When deaths came hard on the heels of one another, when too many patients were panicked and distressed, the staff members would quietly collapse in the locker rooms, ready to throw in the towel.

For my grandparents, the hospital ward, so far away from the village and its gossip, was like a break. A break during which they no longer had to lie, to shore up a family reputation that had no meaning. Having spent a lifetime making a name for themselves out in the valleys, here they felt close to complete strangers. Gay men, drug addicts, haemophiliacs and their families. People they would never otherwise have met. Strangers going through the same ordeal as they were. Strangers to whom they suddenly felt much closer than they did to members of their family. Strangers whose experiences mirrored their tragedy in every detail. Only with these people could my grandmother escape her denial, her loneliness, for a time. Since, like my grandmother, these families were coming during hospital visiting hours, meeting at the same coffee machine, struggling to cope with increasingly complex diagnoses, they were the only people who could understand how she felt. When they passed in the hospital corridor, they greeted each other silently, looked at each other courteously. These people were just as dumbstruck, just as suffocated by years of shame, humiliation and grief that no drug could cure.

# CICLOSPORIN

On Tuesday, 29 October 1985, at 4 p.m., three doctors from Laennec hospital hold a press conference in Paris. The event is significant, all the more so since it has been organized by the Ministry of Health. Dozens of reporters from television, radio and newspapers are in attendance. In a packed lecture hall, the doctors explain that they have had promising results by treating patients with the LAV virus with ciclosporin, a drug primarily used to reduce the risk of organ rejection after transplant.

Surprising as it may seem, the idea is to destroy what remains of the patient's immune system. An immunosuppressant, it was successfully tested a week earlier on two patients: a thirty-five-year-old man and a twenty-eight-year-old woman. Following treatment, both patients experienced a sharp increase in their T4 cell count.

By evening, the news was being relayed by every major newspaper and television channel.

Researchers at the Institut Pasteur, and at Pitié-Salpêtrière hospital, are struggling to hide their scepticism. The timing of the press conference is particularly difficult. At the Institut Pasteur, 70 per cent of beds are occupied by patients suffering from AIDS. On average, three die every week. The moment a bed is free, it is filled by a new patient who is already at death's door. At Pitié-Salpêtrière hospital, admissions have soared to the point that many patients with a temperature of 40°C are sent back home. Since there are no beds, they are told to return when their temperature reaches 41°C.

The idea of conducting trials using ciclosporin to fight AIDS was first raised at the Institut Pasteur in early September 1983. In collaboration with their American colleagues and those at Saint-Louis hospital, David Klatzmann and his team studied the effects of ciclosporin on infected T4 lymphocytes in vitro, but met with disappointing results and did not pursue the research.

David Klatzmann finds the press conference astonishing. The findings directly contradict his own research, and the results on which the three doctors at Laennec are relying seem tenuous at best. The ciclosporin trial involves only two patients, and only a week has passed since treatment began. Why stage a press conference so precipitously? And why is the government, in the person of the Minister for Health, lending such credence to the trial?

Klatzmann and his colleagues will never know.

A few days after the dramatic announcement, the two patients treated with ciclosporin die. And with them die the hopes of many patients and their families who, in this morbid climate, clung to the fantastical promises of three reckless doctors.

# LEAD

In the last weeks of his life, Désiré was all too aware of what lay ahead. The treatments now could do nothing except alleviate his pain. He had watched too many people die not to know that he was nearing the end.

There were fewer visitors at his bedside. Except for Louise and Brigitte, who took turns. Émile would sometimes come on Sunday afternoons. Whatever the state of his brother's health, my father never visited the hospital. Nor did most of Désiré's friends. They were in no rush to see the fate that lay in store for them. As a result of my grandmother's embargo, many in the village did not even know that Désiré was ill. The only people who knew what was happening were those closest to him.

Whenever Brigitte would try to give him a little hope, my uncle would flinch. 'I'm not going to pull through this time. I'm not really sad for myself, it's Émilie. I wanted her to have her father around at least till she was eighteen. If it wasn't for her, I'd have gone out and bought a couple of grams of high-grade smack a long time ago and shot up the whole lot. Bang. End of story. At least I wouldn't be here, coughing my lungs up in front of doctors who give me dirty looks and nurses who are too scared to touch me.'

Désiré was increasingly indifferent to his own fate, and much more worried about Brigitte and Émilie. Perhaps he hoped they would live long enough to benefit from treatment. Perhaps he dreamed of starting over with them, without the drugs, the needles, the disease.

Our family archives censored the end of his life. All that was ever said was that Désiré died of a pulmonary embolism one morning in April 1987. This was what my grandmother always said when she was asked how her son died. She presented a consequence of his illness as the only reason for his death. It didn't matter that it was only a half-truth. For a long time, as far as she was concerned, it would be the only truth about her son's death. A whole truth.

The shame my grandmother had endured up to that terrible day did not end when her son breathed his last breath, when his heart and brain gave out. All too soon, Louise realized that she would have to face yet more humiliations. The first was when the undertakers refused to dress the body in the suit his family had brought from the village for the funeral. Shortly before Désiré's death, the government issued regulations stating that undertakers could not handle the bodies of those who had died of AIDS. The staff at the funeral home had refused to do so anyway. Not only would my uncle not be dressed in fresh clothes before he was buried, but his face would not be made up and there would be no embalming to slow the process of decomposition. My grandmother's pleas were met by the full force of the law. No one was allowed to see Désiré – a prisoner of his lead-lined coffin – to say goodbye. The very earth would not touch his body, would not return him to the dust to which we thought all men returned.

My only memory of Désiré dates from a few months before his death. It is a very brief scene. He is lying in bed in the hospital room to which my grandmother has brought my brother, Émilie and me. All I remember is his weary smile behind the moustache and his frail body shrouded by the sheets. I can see us chatting to him for a while, then each of us kissing him goodbye.

My brother insists that he has no memory of this. His mind has preserved a different image, one of a family meal at our grandparents' house. The adults enjoying a lengthy meal while the children play around the coffee table in the living room. Only Désiré takes no part in the conversations. He stares into the middle distance, half-buried in a huge velvet armchair. He no longer has the strength to eat, he is simply putting in an appearance. He is not yet thirty, but he is the family invalid. My grandmother, who still refuses to admit that he is dying, vainly insists that he eat a little something. As though that would get him back on his feet.

These two memories and a few of our father's Super-8 reels are all we have left of our uncle.

Désiré was buried on the hill outside the village a few days after he died. Leaving the little church, the funeral procession slowly wound its way up to the tiny cemetery.

Standing apart from the family, hidden behind their dark glasses, some of his friends struggled to look upon the fate the virus had in store for them.

The death notice published in *Nice-Matin* the day before did not mention the cause of death. It simply said that his parents, Louise and Émile, his wife Brigitte and his daughter Émilie were 'deeply saddened to announce the death of Désiré, at the tender age of thirty, following a long illness'.

# PART TWO
*Émilie*

# THE ROAD

Every day, come sunshine, rain or snow, a battered blue Citroën C15 made its way down the winding road from the Var valley to Nice. It did not come back until late evening. Behind the wheel, the lady wearing glasses was so small that she could barely see the road over the dashboard.

My grandmother had been up since well before dawn so the butcher's shop would be ready to open on the dot of seven o'clock. At noon, she would help my father and grandfather close up, and the shop would reopen at 3.30 p.m. Without even taking a moment to have lunch, she would set off in the early afternoon to see her granddaughter at Lenval paediatric hospital.

Like Émilie's maternal grandmother, Louise was determined to visit her granddaughter every day when she was in hospital. Both women were honouring promises they had made to Désiré and Brigitte. It was these appointments that stopped them going under after their children died. For the rest of their lives, the two grandmothers cared more about their granddaughter than they did about themselves. They were not the kind of women to give up. Having spent years at the bedside of a sick son and daughter, they had one last battle to fight.

Émilie was like every other child her age. She attended the village school and was no different from her classmates. However, she had to make regular trips to the hospital for check-ups and blood tests. During her early years, she was in good health. Doctors hoped that she might be one of those patients they called 'healthy carriers', those who did not go on to develop AIDS. Her grandmothers, both strong women, raised her with boundless energy. Louise looked after her during school term and her maternal grandmother took her during the holidays. Each had created a bedroom for her in their house.

In the butcher's shop, one of the back rooms had been turned into a playroom. The recess under the stairs was filled with dolls, and Émilie would play there after school if she wasn't hurtling down the rue du 4-Septembre on a skateboard with the neighbourhood kids. My grandmother was worried that she might hurt herself, but could not dampen her enthusiasm.

Over time, Émilie increasingly suffered from fatigue. She began to lose weight and to develop the opportunistic infections typical of the disease, which required her to have longer and more frequent spells in hospital. Like her father and mother before her, she was gradually uprooted from her daily routine, from her village. While other children grew, she seemed to shrink.

Several years had passed since her parents' deaths, and

still doctors had not discovered a drug capable of eliminating the virus in her veins. History was repeating itself. My grandmother drew her strength from the medical check-ups and from her granddaughter's fighting spirit, which she fuelled with sweets, videos and magazines. No matter the state of the mountain roads or her own health, my grandmother would not allow a single day to pass without visiting Émilie. She made sure she talked about the future, told Émilie that one day she would go to the seaside, go skiing or whatever she wanted to do, promised her all the things she needed to cling to life. It was important to hang on until the next illness, to hope, to wait for a cure. Louise would sit by Émilie's bed until the last possible moment, then climb back into her car. There was an hour's drive ahead of her. Sixty-five kilometres of hairpin bends, of steep gorges and rocky roads before she reached the village. At nightfall, exhausted, she would pull into the deserted little square in front of the church. Only the way she walked, now that no one could see, betrayed something of her anguish.

# HIV-2

French researchers quickly became aware that the virus could mutate. As early as 1983, Christine Katlama, an infectious disease specialist working with Willy Rozenbaum at Claude-Bernard hospital, was puzzled by one of her patients, a young man from Cape Verde who had symptoms consistent with infection by the AIDS virus. But he had repeatedly tested negative using the screening tools available at the time.

In 1985, she approaches Christine Rouzioux and Françoise Brun-Vézinet to re-examine the case. She is hoping that the more advanced tests developed by her colleagues will shed more light on the problem. But once again, despite the incontrovertible symptoms, the results are negative.

During a conference in Brussels, Christine Rouzioux has a glimmering of an explanation. She attends a talk given by a colleague, Francis Barin, who shares his experiences and his uncertainties. Barin, a virologist from the University of Tours, believes there is a second virus affecting Senegalese prostitutes. Back in Paris, Rouzioux contacts Christine

Katlama. She thinks that her patient may have been infected by a second strain of the virus now known as HIV for 'Human Immunodeficiency Virus'.

That same year, Luc Montagnier's team gets a phone call from Lisbon. Dr Maria Odette Santos Ferreira is dealing with a number of patients from Cape Verde and Guinea-Bissau, all of whom have the characteristic symptoms of AIDS, but, despite repeated tests, all the results are negative. To try to clear up this mystery, Montagnier invites her to bring the blood samples to Paris.

At the Institut Pasteur, these blood samples are used to isolate a second strain. Genome sequencing reveals it to be significantly different from the strain of HIV that has been used to develop all existing screening tests. Françoise Barré-Sinoussi cultures this second strain in order to study it more closely. Her conclusions are clear: it is a different virus, though one that clearly belongs to the same group as HIV. As researchers at the Institut Pasteur and around the world suspected, the virus is evolving. There is an urgent need to develop new tests capable of detecting both strains of the virus. With the help of Françoise Barré-Sinoussi, Luc Montagnier discovers that those infected with HIV-2 also develop AIDS.

Shortly afterwards, Christine Katlama and Françoise Barré-Sinoussi fly to Cape Verde to study the extent of the epidemic there. They discover the poor sanitation and fragile medical infrastructure conducive to the spread of the virus. It soon becomes clear that the main locus of this second strain will be West Africa.

On Wednesday, 27 January 1988, the CDC in Atlanta reports on the first patient to be diagnosed with AIDS due to HIV-2 infection in Newark, New Jersey. She is a young woman from West Africa.

# THE SCHOOL

Despite the fact that Émilie's health meant that she shuttled back and forth between her family and the hospital, she was still attending the village school. In photos from that time, she can be seen happily posing with the other children. In class, teachers were kind to her. They made sure that, despite her prolonged absences, she was well integrated with her group. Her school records contained a note from doctors stipulating what to do in the event of her suffering injury, fatigue or illness. The teachers were discreet, and never talked about her health. But in such a small community, given the early deaths of her parents, the secret in her blood could not be kept for ever.

When Émilie was at nursery school, a woman circulated a petition among the parents of other children. Her son was in the same class as Émilie and she demanded that the little girl no longer be allowed to attend. In her petition she explained that this would avoid any risk of infection. That year, Émilie's teacher happened to be the head of the school. He refused to give in to pressure. He made it clear that Émilie did not represent a danger to anyone, and that she belonged in school with the other children. No one ever told my cousin about this attempt to get her excluded. My parents and my grandparents were shocked by this incident. It made them realize how difficult it would be to protect Émilie in the years ahead.

In primary school, some of the friends she had played with for years suddenly distanced themselves. They had heard their parents arguing and stopped including Émilie in their games. When Émilie tried to insist, they told her that she had AIDS and they didn't want to be around her because she was infectious. Not only did my cousin not understand what any of this had to do with her, she had probably never heard the disease mentioned other than on television. Her friends took it upon themselves to explain. It was a serious, even fatal disease. Her mother and father had got it from taking drugs; they had died of AIDS, but they had given it to her before they died. Panicked, Émilie admitted that she was more delicate than the other children, that she often got sick and had to go to hospital for treatment, but it had nothing to do with AIDS. As she had so often been told at home, she would be cured soon. But despite her denials, that day none of the children were prepared to believe the story her family had concocted to make her life more bearable.

Émilie went home to her grandmother in tears and told her what had happened. Louise was furious. After reassuring her granddaughter with half-truths and euphemisms, she picked up her phone. The numbers for almost everyone in the village took up just a page and a half in the telephone directory. Before her granddaughter had had time to dry her tears, Louise had called the parents of her classmates to demand an apology. She screamed down the phone, insisting that they come round and tell her granddaughter they were wrong, that she wasn't infectious, that she didn't have AIDS, that she would soon be cured.

Some hours later, a few embarrassed families showed up at the door. This was my grandmother's last stand: she was determined to protect her granddaughter from reality. Powerless in the face of the relentless progress of the disease, she was fighting to save what could still be saved: the semblance of a normal life for Émilie.

# HIV 87

In July 1987, the clinical trial known as HIV 87 begins in Paris. The trial includes 1,650 patients and its goal is to measure the efficacy and toxicity of a much-heralded drug, sodium diethyldithiocarbamate.

INIT 83, a trial carried out in 1983, involved treating six patients with ditiocarb sodium, known as Imuthiol. Initial results were promising. There followed more trials, with larger groups of patients, both in Europe and the United States.

The HIV 87 trial is the most ambitious of all. Imuthiol will be administered once a week to HIV-positive volunteers over the course of two years. Throughout the trial, scientists focus on three criteria: clinical progression of the disease, mortality rates and changes in T4 cells.

As is usual in the case of a double-blind trial, half of the patients will be given a placebo.

On 27 March 1991, the *Journal of the American Medical Association* publishes promising results from a study on ditiocarb sodium therapy conducted by Professor Evan Hersch. The results receive significant press coverage all over the world. Immediately afterwards, the Pasteur-Mérieux laboratory announce that the French Ministry of Health has authorized them to prescribe the drug, which has been the focus of so much hope.

Yet, four months later, despite the promising initial figures published in the American journal, they discover that clinical progression of the disease is more advanced in patients treated with Imuthiol than in those given a placebo. There is no significant difference in T4 cell counts between the two groups. This is all the more disappointing given that the trial monitored patients over a relatively long period.

On 23 July 1991, Pasteur-Mérieux issues a press release – without informing doctors or patients – that it is unilaterally withdrawing the drug. The very next day, the telephone lines of 'SIDA Info Service' are flooded with calls from patients terrified about the potentially dangerous effects of a drug they have been taking for months. Patients and their families, disappointed that the hopes raised by Imuthiol have been dashed, feel abandoned. Of the various political action groups campaigning on AIDS at the time, the most pugnacious is ACT UP Paris, founded two years earlier by Didier Lestrade and modelled on ACT UP New York. Lestrade condemns the fact that no press conference was organized for journalists and association representatives to explain the sudden withdrawal of Imuthiol.

It is all the more surprising given that the drug, which has never been shown to be effective in vitro, has been the subject of clinical trials for almost eight years. Eight years of waiting, of questioning, of vain hopes that crystallize the suffering of patients whose despair seems never-ending.

# SILENCE

Just as Désiré's illness had never been talked about, the family never mentioned his daughter's illness. With her parents now forever asleep, no one even named the poison that coursed through Émilie's veins, although they probably thought about it every day as they stared into space, in the light that streamed through a window. They worried about the future in silence. Tried to come up with answers for the little girl's questions. Questions that became increasingly insistent as she grew older and the virus began to awaken. As she looked at the photographs of her parents on the nightstand, Émilie began to formulate specific questions. But despite her desperate need to understand, and the rumours circulating at school, the family held firm.

On Saturday nights, my brother and I would sometimes go to sleep over at our grandparents' place while our parents went to a friend's house for dinner. My mother would bring us to the butcher's shop in the afternoon. Then, when the shutters came down, she and my father would head out. We would play with Émilie while my grandmother made dinner and my grandfather cleaned the shop for the Sunday morning reopening. We would eat in the kitchen in the back of the shop with my grandparents and Émilie, who was thrilled to have company.

After dinner, we would walk to 'the store', my grandparents' house. Before curling up under a blanket and falling asleep to a Disney video, we would make the most of the short walk to look up at the stars. Émilie would often point to two of the brightest stars. She said they were her parents looking down on us. When I pointed out that this didn't square with what we had been taught about the stars and the solar system at school, my grandmother would back up Émilie. This was the family myth about her parents. She had been told that, when they were very young, they had got sick and left to join the stars that rose above the dark mountains in the blue nights of summer.

One day while my brother and I were killing time with a friend, standing on the bridge, spitting into the river, our friend mentioned our cousin. He had been wondering whether we knew that she had AIDS. I was disgusted by this question. It was not the first time I had heard the term AIDS, but previously it had always been associated with homosexuals and drug addicts. I told him point-blank: my cousin wasn't a homosexual or a junkie. She hadn't got AIDS. I reeled off the family sermon: Émilie had a serious illness, but doctors would cure it eventually. In my friend's eyes I saw a flicker of embarrassment. Not only did he not believe me, but he seemed sorry, heartbroken, that I was one of the few people who still believed my story.

As soon as I got home, I ran into the kitchen to tell my mother about this weird conversation. After a long sigh, she set down the kitchen knife and, without looking up from the countertop, she said, yes. Émilie had AIDS. But, although this was true, I should never, under any circumstances, tell Émilie. There was no point in telling her now, after years of struggle. It would only frighten her, make her lose hope. It was important that she not give up, that she keep fighting. This was the kind of disease that would consume you if you gave in to it. I raised the same objection I had with my friend a few minutes earlier: my cousin couldn't have caught AIDS at her age, she wasn't homosexual, she wasn't a drug addict. It didn't make sense.

She had caught it from her parents. This is what my mother told me. Désiré and Brigitte had used needles to inject drugs. They had become infected through using those needles. And when Brigitte got pregnant, she passed the disease on to Émilie.

In three sentences, my mother had just passed on my share of the family burden. Her answers brought with them a torrent of questions that I could not ask. She was sapped by what she had just told me. Suddenly I saw my memories in a different light: how thin Brigitte had been the last times we had seen her in the village, how thin Désiré was in the family photos, my father's clenched jaw when I mentioned Amsterdam, my mother's worry every time Émilie scratched herself playing in the garden, her panic at the trickling blood, all these wounds that had to be healed whatever the costs.

# CONCORDE

In 1987, an American study puts forward evidence for the efficacy of AZT in patients in the advanced stages of AIDS. However, in France and the United Kingdom there are still reservations about the effectiveness of the drug, especially in asymptomatic patients – those who are HIV-positive but have not yet developed AIDS. Needless to say, the American study shows a clear rise in the T4 cell count in most patients. But there are insufficient retrospective or statistical studies to determine the long-term efficacy of AZT on patient mortality.

In 1988, French and British researchers launch the Concorde trial, the largest ever clinical trial of AZT. Concorde sets out to study the course of HIV infection in 1,749 HIV-positive people in hospitals throughout France and the UK. The aim is to test the long-term effects of the drug. This mammoth trial will run for more than five years.

For their part, the Americans are somewhat dismissive of the European trial, based as it is on a long-term methodology and indicators they consider outdated.

In French and British clinics, the patients are divided into two groups. In the asymptomatic phase, the first will be given zidovudine (AZT), while the second will be given a placebo. Once a patient develops AIDS, they are given AZT regardless of the group to which they were initially assigned.

On 2 April 1993, the results of the Concorde trial are published in *The Lancet*. This marks the end of a period of doubt in which the hopes of many patients have taken refuge. The figures are unarguable: after five years, and despite a significant rise in the T4 cell count of those treated, mortality in the group immediately given AZT is 8 per cent, and 7 per cent in the group who were given AZT only after they developed the disease. The verdict is clear: there is no significant benefit to the early treatment of asymptomatic patients. Contrary to popular belief, AZT prescribed before the onset of the disease does not slow the progress of the virus or prolong life. Above all, the toxic side effects of AZT have tarnished its image as a miracle drug.

Burroughs Wellcome, which has attempted to challenge the legitimacy of the Concorde trial, sees the value of its shares plummet within minutes.

In France, there is a huge outcry because the 14,000 people being treated with AZT learn about the outcome of the trial from *The Lancet* via the media, before the ANRS (the French national AIDS research agency) even has time to publish a statement.

After the successive failures of HPA-23 and Imuthiol, followed by the hasty withdrawal of the latter, the sense of despair is growing.

# DEAD END

It was 1994, the year Émilie turned ten, that saw the tipping point the family had been dreading ever since she was born. The dormant virus had not awakened overnight. For several years, her bouts of illness had grown more frequent and more severe. But it was at the dawn of her second short decade that the virus got the upper hand.

Up to this point, the doctor treating her had been satisfied with the results of AZT. While hardly inspiring, their analyses showed that the drug was reasonably effective. It seemed to bolster Émilie's immune system. But in her case, as in that of so many other patients, the effects of zidovudine were eventually wiped out.

Doctors informed the family that there was no other treatment. The only thing they could do was alleviate her pain. They had all come to a dead end: the doctors with the family, the family with the little girl. The family knew little about virology, but they understood. This was the third time this tragedy had befallen them. Regardless of advancements in research, Émilie was doomed to the same fate as her father and mother.

So they had to come up with some reason to stand with

her and fight, some reason to believe. Not because there had to be a reason somewhere in the universe, but because there was no alternative. The situation required them to hope in a world with no hope, to plan in a world with no future, to fight on in a world with no possibility of victory. This was their role from now on: to pointlessly carry on.

No one shirked the task. Everyone was heroic. Not in the way you see in Hollywood movies. Everyone played their part right to the end, humble, helpless characters in an absurd plot where nothing was at stake. A world in which there was nothing left to save. My grandmother spent more time than ever with her granddaughter. My grandfather was at her bedside as often as he could be. For Émilie's sake, he gave up the long drives through the valley that had kept him going. My parents, my uncles and my aunt took it in turns to go to Nice and be with her. Sitting by her bed, they would encourage her to eat, talk to her about the future. They would come back to the village late at night, exhausted and desperate. But, like the nursing staff and their close friends, they knew only one thing for certain: the battle had been lost.

Terrified by her illness, my brother and I refused to sit with Émilie. Our parents were torn. On the one hand, they wanted to protect us, but on the other, they wanted Émilie to see her cousins. For a while, my father found a way to coerce us. Every Sunday, he would offer to take us to the cinema in Nice. Since there was only one screening a week in the village hall, usually an adult film, this was bound to appeal to us.

After the movie, as he pulled out of the underground car park, he would tell us that we should make the most of the opportunity to see our cousin. As he drove the battered old Ford down the Promenade des Anglais towards the hospital, it was too late for us to escape. As the lift slowly rose from floor to floor, I would try to catch my father's eye, pleading with him not to make us do this.

Over the weeks, my parents realized just how difficult we were finding the situation too. They stopped forcing us to visit our cousin. My father would sometimes still take us to the cinema before going to the hospital. But when we got to Émilie's ward, he would sigh and tell us we could wait for him by the lifts. Then he would disappear behind a door into a room a few metres away. While he was visiting, we would spend the whole time staring guiltily at our trainers.

The last time we went to the hospital, I remember we bumped into Émilie's maternal grandmother. She had just left her granddaughter chatting with her uncle. She was surprised to see us there, and, like our father, urged us to go sit with our cousin. I remember two boys, backed up against the door of the lift, more intimidated than they were by their father's plea, mutely shaking their heads.

On the way home, no one would say anything. We made the most of those drives to listen to radio stations we couldn't get in the village. Occasionally an old stand-up routine by Coluche would wrest a burst of laughter from my father, and set us free: 'Fucking hell, he's an idiot!'

The radio would fade to static as we neared the valleys, giving way to silence. We could see nothing but the darkness and ropes of street lamps strung over the black hulk of the mountains. To rip open this silence, I would ask my father what some light on the dashboard was for, or the name of some village glittering in the distance. The longer the questions went on, the longer his answers became. He would start by explaining the workings of the car and end by recounting childhood memories of travelling in the butcher's van with his father. We were warmed by his words. We would listen, our faces pressed against the windows. These conversations were our way of reconnecting, of recapturing the humdrum of life after facing something that looked terrifyingly like death.

As her health deteriorated, Émilie's comings and goings between the village and the hospital came to an end. The little girl now never left Lenval, not even for special occasions, family celebrations or birthdays. The paediatric hospital had become her last domain, her home, her school, her whole world. A tiny universe, from whose windows she could see the cars along the Promenade des Anglais, the carefree ramblers and the vast expanse of the azure sea. The world continued to turn, but to her, it was now inaccessible, irrelevant.

One day, while she was still questioning the family about how she came to be ill, she sighed and whispered that if her parents hadn't done 'stupid stuff', she wouldn't have had to go through all this. How much had she truly understood? Everything, probably. She would surely have remembered the gossip she'd heard in the playground and the village streets. In the privacy of her hospital room, all these stories finally resurfaced.

All therapeutic treatments had been discontinued and Émilie was now being given more and more drugs to alleviate her pain. Some caused her face to swell. She was taking so many drugs now that she lost what little appetite she still had. She was getting thinner and thinner.

She often asked to see her cousins, who no longer came to visit. The younger ones risked bringing in some innocuous illness that could prove fatal to her. The older ones, despite their parents' repeated entreaties, were terrified that they would see in her the ghost of the cousin they had known.

# DELTA

In the early 1990s, researchers are looking for more effective treatments to replace AZT, which has serious side effects. Around the world, scientists are taking advantage of the availability of new drugs to test them against the virus. The results of these trials are eagerly awaited, now that the Concorde trial has dashed patients' hopes.

Not that they have given up prescribing AZT. Despite the serious side effects, it has proven effective at boosting T4 cell counts in patients and temporarily strengthening their immune systems. But it is now prescribed in lower doses. The paucity of early studies meant that doses prescribed until now were too high, gravely exacerbating the side effects without improving therapeutic benefits. Researchers are now seeking to combine AZT with other drugs to address its limitations.

This is the context in which Christine Katlama, with the help of colleagues at Pitié-Salpêtrière hospital, begins trialling a combination of AZT and 3TC. At this point, Glaxo Wellcome (a merger of the Burroughs Wellcome and Glaxo laboratories) is on the point of discontinuing production of 3TC since it shows no significant effect on T4 cell counts.

But an initial in-vitro trial at Pitié-Salpêtrière offers more encouraging results. In viral cultures, the AZT-3TC combination works.

In order to save time, Christine Katlama suggests relatively flexible clinical trials. She manages to convince Glaxo Wellcome not to stop production of 3TC so that she can carry out a large-scale trial on volunteer patients.

After six months of treatment, the mortality rate falls and the health of her patients improves somewhat. As the young infectious disease specialist is presenting these results at a conference in Glasgow, she sees in the eyes of the audience a new glimmer of hope.

This period also sees the start of the Delta trial, spearheaded by Jean-Paul Lévy and Maxime Seligmann, which brings together the ANRS in France and the British Medical Research Council. Once again, the aim is to trial a combination regimen of AZT and another drug – didanosine (ddI) or zalcitabine (ddC) – on more than 3,000 symptomatic and asymptomatic patients.

The first group, known as Delta 1, consists of 1,083 patients who are referred to as 'naive', meaning they have not previously been treated with AZT. The second, Delta 2, comprises 2,131 non-naive patients who have already had antiretroviral therapy. After twenty-six months, the findings presented on 13 September 1995 are so conclusive that the steering committee immediately recommends that the trial be abandoned.

The first finding is that participants in both groups were

highly likely to prematurely discontinue trial therapy. Taken on its own, AZT caused serious side effects. In combination with a second drug, these effects proved even more difficult for patients to tolerate. Almost two-thirds of patients discontinued therapy during the trial, largely of their own volition. Nonetheless, in the Delta 1 group there is a clear reduction in the mortality rate among those who were able to continue combination therapy. Mortality in this group appears to have fallen by 38 per cent. Results in the Delta 2 group are much less encouraging. Combination therapy offered no advantages in terms of mortality or life expectancy to patients who had already taken antiretroviral medications.

The results of the Delta trial and the trial at Pitié-Salpêtrière hospital demonstrate the importance of prescribing AZT as part of a combination regimen, rather than in isolation. For the first time, studies confirm that combining zidovudine with another drug delays the complications associated with infection and significantly extends the life expectancy of patients.

# GOD THE FATHER

I don't know whether my mother ever actually believed in God. I don't think she ever managed to. Her rare moments of faith collided with the harsh realities of the world. And, in fact, it was my brother and I who asked if we could enrol in the weekly catechism class given by the village priest during lunch hour. Most of our friends attended and we found ourselves at a loose end in the playground.

I remember the lessons always followed the exact same pattern. The priest would read a passage from the Bible or tell us a religious story, then he would hand out colouring books that illustrated the story. Once, he told us about Lourdes. We were spellbound by this miraculous grotto and its spring, especially because it still seemed to be active, and it was only a few hundred kilometres from where we lived.

That night, when my mother came home from work, I ran over to tell her the story of this grotto with a bubbling spring in a small town in the Pyrenees called Lourdes. It had the power to cure diseases for which there was no cure. People arrived on crutches and left there running. At first, my mother listened distractedly while she put the groceries in the kitchen cupboards. It was only when I suggested that we take my cousin there to be cured that she lost her temper. She told me that Émilie had drunk litres and litres of Lourdes water. That every time some villager visited Lourdes, they'd bring her back a little plastic bottle of water in the shape of the Virgin Mary and it had never done any good. It was all bullshit.

I bowed my head and headed off to do my homework. She caught up with me in the hall and apologized for getting angry. It had been a lovely, kind idea, but they had tried it already. It was sweet of me to think of it, she said.

During my childhood, I often heard my mother say that now was not the time to talk to her about God, that all the religious claptrap in the world hadn't done a thing to prevent the deaths of my uncle, my aunt and my cousin. She used to say that if there really was a God, he wouldn't allow such things to happen. Her convictions wavered only during funerals, when grief drove her to a very personal kind of mysticism. One night, sitting in front of the television, she called the Pope a 'moron'. At the height of the AIDS epidemic, John Paul II had opposed the use of condoms.

Every Sunday morning during my cousin's last summer, my mother would wake us at nine o'clock. She would ask us to go to mass and pray for Émilie. She said it probably wouldn't do any good, but it was the only thing left that we could do.

# MOTHER-TO-CHILD TRANSMISSION

The year 1987 sees the start of the first French studies of HIV-positive pregnant women. For a long time, the mechanisms of mother-to-child transmission will puzzle scientists, making it very difficult to prevent. Studies of foetal tissue from first-trimester abortions rarely show any signs of infection. As a result, researchers assume that infection usually occurs during the third trimester, rather than in the early months of pregnancy. Gradually, they identify a number of other ways in which the virus might pass from mother to child: during labour, during delivery, or during breastfeeding.

In the early 1990s, researchers note that the onset of the disease in children seems to vary according to the stage of pregnancy when transmission occurred. AIDS seems to develop very quickly in children infected around the second trimester, whereas in those infected late in the pregnancy, the advancement is much slower and similar to that in adults.

Initial tests are carried out in mice in an attempt to understand the mechanism of transmission. Various drugs that might potentially hinder transmission are tested. In this particular field, it is very difficult to carry out tests on human subjects, for technical and ethical reasons.

The clinical trials ACTG 076/ANRS 024 begin in the United States in 1991, and in France in 1993. The French trial is led by Professor Jean-François Delfraissy under the aegis of Inserm and the ANRS. Delfraissy is an immunologist at Kremlin-Bicêtre hospital in Paris, where the death toll has been calamitous: some 120 deaths a year. The atmosphere is grim.

The ACTG 076/ANRS 024 trials involve giving AZT to the mother during the pregnancy and to the child during its first weeks. Researchers are studying the clinical efficacy of AZT in preventing perinatal transmission.

The 477 women enrolled in the study are divided into two groups. Those in the first group are treated with AZT, while those in the second are given a placebo. Similarly, after birth, only a percentage of newborns will receive AZT.

Initial results are promising. Of the 415 babies born before the cut-off date, the HIV status of 363 is known. Researchers note a rate of transmission in the AZT-treated group of around 8 per cent, as compared to 25 per cent in the group receiving the placebo. The drug has proved effective in limiting the risk of transmission from a pregnant mother to her child. The results are so encouraging that the ethics committee decides to discontinue the trial for those patients receiving the placebo so they can be given AZT.

The data is made public in February 1994. At about this time, the World Health Organization resolves to develop an international strategy in this field.

# NINJA TURTLES

By summer's end, it had been many weeks since Émilie had last been able to leave her hospital room. Special permission was given for her to return to her family in the village. The girl was a shadow of her former self. Pale and gaunt, she could not take even a few steps without support. But she didn't complain. She seemed resigned to a body that now denied her all the things it had once allowed.

While our parents had eventually agreed that my brother and I no longer had to visit her in hospital, for this special occasion, my mother gave us no choice. The ambulance bringing Émilie home was due to arrive in the village mid-afternoon. My mother told us to be back from the local swimming pool by 4 p.m. so we could spend some time with Émilie.

I can't remember ever being late in my childhood, except that day. My brother and I deliberately did not look at the clock above the lifeguard's chair. We hoped we would arrive home too late. At 4.30 p.m., my mother appeared outside the perimeter fence. We couldn't hide any longer. On the drive home, she could barely contain her anger. She insisted on the gravity of the situation, reminded us that this was probably one of the last evenings we would get to share with our cousin. My brother and I were only just eleven but we felt completely contemptible.

Émilie was waiting in the room where we used to play. Like the hospital corridor some months earlier, the hall in our house seemed never-ending. When we went into the room, she was quietly waiting, staring straight ahead of her at the switched-off television.

In the oppressive silence, we sat down next to her. My brother and I suggested playing Ninja Turtles, a Nintendo game she loved. Since her last visit to the village, we had made a lot of progress. But Émilie didn't seem particularly impressed by the graphics in the last few levels. The tinny sounds from the Nintendo console took the place of conversation. My brother and I would hand her the controller so she could play, but she no longer had the strength even for that. Her eyes moved frantically over the garishly coloured pixels on the screen, no longer excited by the worlds they depicted. The disease had robbed her of her childhood. All the things that had once captivated or delighted her now evoked only sighs of indifference.

When she grew tired of the two of us glancing at her surreptitiously, Émilie eventually asked my mother if there was somewhere she could lie down. My mother put her in my room, where she fell asleep.

Émilie had come to play with us one last time and, despite the importance of the situation, we hadn't been able to get her to join in our game. The people, the places, the furniture were all still there, but they seemed to elude her. Even the

## SLEEPING CHILDREN

two cousins with whom she'd spent countless afternoons roaming the village streets and countless nights watching dumb cartoons only reminded her of a life that was slipping away.

When she woke up, she asked my mother to take her to our grandparents' house.

# STALINGRAD

In March 1995, at Garches hospital, Jacques Leibowitch is not about to shut up. He was the first person in France to suggest that AIDS might be caused by a retrovirus. He has lost nothing of his fiery temperament. He is busy telling anyone who will listen that he literally spelled out the word *retrovirus* to Willy Rozenbaum over lunch at the Closerie des Lilas. Later, he had a falling out with Rozenbaum and worked more closely with the Americans, while Rozenbaum sought help from the Institut Pasteur.

Everyone in the research community agrees: Leibowitch is capable of the best and the worst, of towering rages and dazzling flashes of genius. So, while his tantrums have left him somewhat isolated within the scientific community, his extraordinary intelligence has enabled him to make progress in his research. When he was unable to agree with the majority of the French pioneers researching the virus, he stormed out of the French AIDS Working Group despite having attended its inaugural meeting in spring 1982, when there were only about twenty cases of AIDS in France. Like the researchers at the Institut Pasteur, he has regularly published his findings and has collaborated with Robert

Gallo's team. But he was too hasty in endorsing the theory that AIDS was caused by an HTLV retrovirus at a time when his colleagues at the Institut Pasteur were discovering the new retrovirus, LAV, later renamed HIV.

This early error didn't stop him from being one of the first scientists capable of manually detecting the virus in blood samples – particularly those intended for transfusions – before the Institut Pasteur developed ELISA. Like his colleagues at the Institut, Leibowitch tried to alert the Ministry of Social Affairs to the dangers faced by those receiving blood transfusions. Now, as a new century dawns, he remains one of the ten French researchers most familiar with AIDS research.

At a time when an average of three people a week are dying in the AIDS ward at the Institut Pasteur, Jacques Leibowitch is continuing his investigations on the outskirts of Paris, in the tranquillity of his laboratory at Raymond-Poincaré University Hospital of Garches. Far from the stressful atmosphere of overcrowded hospitals whose wards have become little more than dying rooms, he is working on his idée fixe: how to wipe out the virus with a cocktail of drugs.

It is an idea that has gradually engrossed him and his colleagues; the results of dual therapies have pointed the way. This line of research has become Leibowitch's obsession, and he refuses to believe that there isn't a weapon capable of destroying the virus. So he spends his time researching, combining, dosing and evaluating drugs. And still the work continues to grow since, by the mid-1990s, more and more drugs are appearing on the market.

He is particularly interested in protease inhibitors, which act at a stage in viral replication on which researchers have so far had little success. The circumstances are more auspicious. With the advancement in tests to detect viral load, thanks to the work of Françoise Brun-Vézinet and Jean Dormont in particular, it is possible to monitor and evaluate the efficacy of a given treatment more accurately than ever, by directly measuring the amount of the virus present in a patient's blood. Prior to this, researchers had to content themselves with calculating the damage caused to the immune system using T4 cell count.

Working with some twenty patients who have already developed AIDS, Leibowitch trials a triple combination therapy consisting of AZT, ddC and ritonavir, a protease inhibitor from Abbott Laboratories in the USA, which he believes to be the most effective of its kind. Leibowitch wants to lay siege to the virus, to declare all-out war, and so he names his trial 'Stalingrad'. Two similar trials are already under way in the United States.

The results of the Stalingrad trial are all the more impressive because they can be seen within a few short months. Having spent more than a decade vainly attempting to stem the mounting death toll, oscillating between failure and false hope, Leibowitch and all his colleagues are stunned. They can scarcely believe it. Yet the results from the first analyses could not be clearer: despite the gruelling nature of the treatment, it has recorded a spectacular fall in viral load in every single patient. At long last.

# THE PENDULUM

Émilie was still gravely ill in mid-October. My parents took it in turns to visit her every night after work and did not return until very late. In the silence and the half-light, they would dine on leftovers and share the latest news. My brother and I would have long since gone to bed. From our bedroom, we couldn't really hear what was being said down in the kitchen. We could just make out our father's stoic whispers and our mother's muffled sobs. When eventually they would come up to kiss us goodnight, we would usually pretend to be asleep, as though to shield ourselves from their despair.

Every day, customers at the butcher's shop would ask for news of 'the little one'. As the crowds filed out from Sunday mass, old ladies would stop by to tell my grandmother that the priest had mentioned Émilie in his sermon and that everyone had prayed for her. At the village school, the teacher suggested pupils in her class send drawings and comforting messages.

It was at about this time that a woman from the village phoned the shop. She had a cousin who was a magnetic healer. He had sometimes healed people that doctors claimed were incurable. She apologized for bothering my grandparents with such a thing, especially given the circumstances. But knowing of their granddaughter's long, lingering agony, she felt it was worth trying something. She told my grandmother that the magnetic healer could work remotely, using photographs of Émilie, but had a better chance of success if he could meet her.

The whole family gathered to come to a decision. My parents certainly gave no more credence to this initiative than they did to the little old ladies in the village who brought holy water from Lourdes. But, if it made my grandmother feel that she was still fighting, they were prepared to go along with it. So my uncles, my aunt and my parents agreed. A meeting was arranged a few days later at the hospital.

That night, shortly before the end of visiting hours, a man in his fifties came to the little girl's hospital room. A few family members who wanted to witness this unusual session were present. The man was given a chair next to the child's bed. After explaining his curious occupation, he suggested we begin.

He laid a hand on Émilie's skeletal body for at least ten minutes, murmuring incantations so quiet they were impossible to hear. With his other hand, he held a shiny brass pendulum that he swung over her. Everyone else in the room was silent and utterly still. After a time, the magnetic healer fell silent. He sat back in his chair, then, in a soothing voice, he broke the silence to tell us that he had finished.

He said goodbye to my cousin, wished her well and praised her for her courage so far. My grandparents walked him down the hospital corridor and thanked him for coming all the way to Nice. The man repeated his message of hope. Before taking his leave, he admitted that his art was far from exact, but that he had felt he had to try. He would carry on working every day at home, using the photo of the child entrusted to him.

A few minutes after he left, a care assistant came to give Émilie her dinner. She ate with a relish no one had seen in months. My grandmother was thrilled to see that she was already recovering her strength.

Despite this moment which seemed suspended in time, the little girl's condition continued to deteriorate. The results of the medical tests carried out over the following days were in no way swayed by the magnetic healing powers of this well-meaning man in his fifties and his little brass pendulum.

# WASHINGTON

In January 1996, a conference in Washington DC is informed of the spectacular results of the two clinical studies using triple combination therapy – including the Stalingrad trial led by Jacques Leibowitch at Garches hospital. The studies used combinations of three very different products. The American trial used AZT, ddI and the protease inhibitor indinavir, while the French combined AZT with ddC and ritonavir. The goal, however, is the same: to destroy the virus in the blood. After fifteen years of research, advances, mistakes, failures and hopes, the results are extremely encouraging.

The papers presented at the Washington congress make it clear that the average viral load detected in the bloodstream can be divided by a figure of between 100 and 1,000 in patients who have not previously had antiretroviral treatment. For the first time at an international conference, it seems possible to be hopeful about the future. Soon, they believe, it will be possible to completely block the HIV replication in those infected.

Despite this undeniable success, there is still much to be done. In all of the trials, about one in four patients discontinued combination therapy, because the side effects were difficult to tolerate. Moreover, the triple combination therapies need to be tested in non-naive patients, i.e. those who have already had antiretroviral treatment.

Doctors are faced with two serious challenges. Firstly, they need to find the combination best suited to each patient; secondly, and more urgently, they need to make these new drugs available to as many people as possible.

# NOVEMBER

One day in November, the phone in our house rang late in the afternoon. My father had rolled down the shutters on the butcher's shop early. Our parents told my brother and me that they were going to drop us off at a friend's house for the night. The following morning, we would probably walk to school with them. The whole family would not be together until sometime that evening. They told us to behave ourselves. Émilie was very poorly. They had to go down to Nice to visit her.

I imagine that my father drove as fast as he could, that they tore down the winding valley roads. I can picture the constellations of small villages glittering in the darkness, the roads glistening with frost, the gleam of headlights. I can see the fog, the steep walls of the dark ravines, and, finally, the sky, as they emerged onto the plains.

I cannot hear anything, except perhaps the purring of the diesel engine in my father's clapped-out Ford that might deaden the silent agony of not getting there in time. My father probably dropped my mother off at the hospital entrance to save a few precious seconds.

But it wasn't enough. They knew it the moment they

stepped onto Émilie's ward. They walked past nurses and orderlies. Those who were not crying stared at their feet by way of condolence. It was all over. They had arrived too late to see her one last time.

Émilie had died. Her body had finally given out. Minutes earlier, she had fallen asleep, surrounded by her grandparents and a number of aunts and uncles. Other family members had raced during the night as soon as they got the news. Waiting in the corridor, their hands behind their backs, leaning against the walls so as not to block the path of the doctors and the nurses, they took it in turns to sit next to Émilie. Out of modesty and a desire not to make too much noise in the sleeping hospital, they huddled together, whispering words of comfort and stifling their sobs.

The virus had reached its absurd conclusion. Contrary to those who referred to it as cunning and malignant, it had killed its host, destroyed her immune system. The virus had brought down the pillars of the sanctuary that would now collapse on it. Once cold, Émilie's body became a dead end. Although it had managed to travel from her father to her mother and from her mother to her, it had found no other ship to destroy. How long would it survive inside her dead body, moving through her veins? A few hours? A few days? No one thought to ask such doleful questions, except the undertakers. They treated Émilie's body as they had treated her parents.

Having spent so many years sitting at the bedside of this little girl as often as they could, no one could bring themselves to leave her hospital room. Some refused to go back to the village without her. Staring out of the window onto the Promenade des Anglais, they stood, silent, motionless, staring out to sea, waiting patiently for dawn to shred the remnants of the night.

# LOTTERY

After the Washington conference, two of the three manufacturers of protease inhibitors, Abbott Laboratories and Merck & Co, issue a statement saying that they cannot produce the drugs quickly enough to satisfy global demand. On both sides of the Atlantic, there is a grave concern they will run out of stock of these new drugs, which are essential to triple combination therapy for patients with HIV. Faced with this possibility, the initial statement from the French Ministry of Health refers simply to a 'disparity between supply and demand'.

On 26 February 1996, the Conseil national du SIDA (National AIDS Council), acting on behalf of the ministry, recommends – provisionally and exceptionally – that HIV-positive people should take part in a lottery to decide who should be treated with the new drug until such times as laboratories can increase production. Unsurprisingly, this suggestion provokes an outcry from patients and organizations. Although the uproar is immense, it goes largely unheard. A majority of doctors, themselves concerned that certain major hospitals are being given more provisions than others, say nothing.

Faced with the demands of AIDS organizations, the Conseil national du SIDA insists that the French government put pressure on the United States to obtain satisfactory quantities of protease inhibitors as quickly as possible. In the meantime, it suggests that priority be given to patients with the weakest immune systems. They envisage earmarking the first available doses of the drug for patients with a T4 cell count of fewer than 100 per cubic millimetre of blood, and, in particular, those with the most worrying clinical signs that the disease is progressing. Simultaneously, the French government announces that, as soon as practicable, it will buy the necessary medications from the United States, and impose no limit on the budget. This, they estimate, will allow them to treat 1,000 new patients each month.

Two days later, on Wednesday, 28 February, Prime Minister Alain Juppé issues a press release definitively ruling out the use of a lottery system. In the end, it will turn out that more drugs are available than was initially thought. The much-feared shortage in France never occurs.

# NOVEMBER (STILL)

I remember almost nothing. I wish I had forgotten what little I do remember. A tiny white coffin, lead-lined like those of her father and her mother. A size of coffin that should not even exist. Even Christ, who is laid to rest at the foot of the cross, on the great wooden carving outside the village church, was allowed time to grow up.

This is all I remember: the dry, bitter cold of a November afternoon and a silent crowd looking the other way when they hear my grandmother howl. At the head of the funeral procession, she is being held up, like a wounded soldier being led back from the front. A day of loss.

In the village, no funeral goes by unmarked. Émilie's funeral brought the whole community together. Shopkeepers rolled down their shutters, children missed school, labourers left their building sites and employees took the afternoon off so they could be on the village square.

Despite the cold, it was impossible to close the church doors that day. Family and friends, neighbours and villagers were joined by many people who travelled up from Nice. Doctors, care workers, the heads of charities helping HIV-positive children, people we did not really know, but who knew Émilie.

During the funeral service, the priest relied on imagery. In his sermon, there was no mention of heroin, AIDS or AZT. Oh, no. He spoke entirely in euphemisms and metaphors. Émilie had gone to join her parents, whom she missed terribly, in a peaceful world where she would no longer have to suffer. Who could believe such things? Had they believed a single word he said, no one would have been so devastated.

The priest recounted Émilie's short life as though everything had been ordained by God. The same God to whom we had so often prayed in vain. The God who insisted that we not question this story, who transformed gratuitous suffering into divine appeals, turned corpses sealed in lead-lined coffins into blessed souls gone to sit at his right hand. Only unutterable grief and deep despair could persuade anyone to believe.

A vast cortège followed the little white coffin up the hill. There were so many people on the narrow road between the church and the cemetery that it looked as though it were overflowing. As the coffin was lowered into the grave, people had to support my grandmother, who still could not accept her failure.

Gently, the child was returned to her parents in a vault that was already overcrowded. It took endless minutes before the mourners dispersed and left the family to grieve.

That night, after the funeral, the family all gathered at my grandparents' house. We all tried to eat or drink something, to comfort each other by passing on words of support and affection we had heard during the day. We made an endless list of the people we had seen, the carers we thought we recognized. We wrote their names in a notebook so we would not forget to thank them.

My father talked to my grandfather about his dogs, while my mother offered my grandmother sleeping pills. After so many years of selflessly devoting themselves to the fight, all they could do now was take care of each other.

AIDS had finished with us. It had gone off to destroy other bodies, to poison other dreams of simple lives. It had left behind only the survivors of a dazed family, offering each other pills that could not even knock them out for a few hours so they might forget the memories that would haunt them for ever.

# EPILOGUE

# NOBEL

On 6 October 2008, Françoise Barré-Sinoussi is in Cambodia taking part in a working meeting about clinical trials on tuberculosis/HIV coinfections. Since the early 2000s, she has been coordinating French–Cambodian bilateral work on HIV/AIDS for France's National Agency for Research on AIDS and Viral Hepatitis. The meeting has already begun when her phone rings. A journalist from Radio France has been trying to get in touch with her, and is surprised that she has got through. She knows the researcher has not yet heard the news, so she tells her. Françoise Barré-Sinoussi has been awarded the Nobel Prize for Medicine, jointly with Luc Montagnier, for their discovery of Human Immunodeficiency Virus at the Institut Pasteur in 1983. French research in the field has finally been recognized at the highest level.

But many people cannot understand the decision to award the prize to only two researchers. Why isn't there a wider attribution? One might think of Willy Rozenbaum, Jacques Leibowitch and Françoise Brun-Vézinet, who sounded the alarm when the disease first appeared and approached the Institut Pasteur; Jean-Claude Chermann, the director of the laboratory where Françoise Barré-Sinoussi worked; and David Klatzmann, the first researcher to observe the action of the virus on T4 cells. People are also surprised that it has taken so long for the French scientists to be acknowledged. According to the Swedish Academy, the twenty-five years that have passed were needed in order to appreciate this discovery in its entirety and over the long term.

In interviews with the media, Françoise Barré-Sinoussi takes the opportunity to recall all those years of research, work, the formal and informal meetings, the international conferences at which she talked to French and foreign colleagues. But when she comes to accept the award, she shares her regret that, despite advances in treatment, the epidemic has still not been eradicated.

The awards ceremony takes place in Stockholm on 10 December 2008. In their speeches, both winners highlight the collaborative nature of the discovery.

# CHAGRIN

No one in the family ever mentioned this story again.

One Sunday, a few months after our cousin's funeral, while my father was putting shelves up in the garage, my brother and I suddenly heard him swearing and smashing the planks of wood, kicking and punching them. He never let go of his anger. One day, he simply walked away from everything: his family, the butcher's shop and the village.

Even today, my mother doesn't talk much. After my father left, she rebuilt her life. All that remains now from that time is a picture frame next to the telephone, which no one is allowed to touch. A picture frame with a photograph of a little girl.

As for my grandmother, although she never talked about it directly, she would often remind me in my early teens to use condoms; she even offered to go to the village pharmacy and buy them for me. It was very important, she said, nothing to be ashamed of. Then, one morning, she woke up coughing blood. The doctor sent her to Nice for tests, which quickly delivered their verdict. She died a few weeks later. In the village, people often said that she was so busy taking care of other people that she forgot to take care of herself.

After Louise died, Émile found himself alone with his dog. Being retired now, this man whose whole life had been devoted to work, devoted himself to his vegetable garden, and gave eggs and vegetables to anyone who wanted them. Like the others, he never talked about the story I have attempted to write. The only way he knew how to express himself was by giving away the produce from his garden and making affectionate jokes.

When he started to lose his sight and his memory, and could no longer work in the garden, he would hobble around the village with his dog. He made the most of any little encounter to have a chat. This man who had known the village when it was a thriving sous-préfecture no longer recognized it, with its boarded-up shops and its streets empty of pedestrians. The old man wandered through the remnants of a world that had died before him. He could often be seen sitting on a bench in the sun. Perhaps he had finally found some kind of peace.

One day, shortly before his death, he asked my brother to help him climb the few steps up to his house. In the confusion inflicted on him by Alzheimer's, he mentioned that he'd just found Désiré sleeping in the street again. When he couldn't wake him he had asked people to help him get his son back to bed.

'He's been injecting himself again. All the things that boy has put us through. Did you know, it's because of the drugs that he caught that bug?'

These were the only words that pierced the armour of his grief.

# ORIGIN

On 3 October 2014, the academic journal *Science* publishes a multi-authored article. An international team, led by Nuno Faria of Oxford University, claims to have pinpointed the historical and geographical origins of the AIDS epidemic. For some years, it has been common knowledge that HIV is a form of virus that migrated from the great apes to humans, during a hunting accident or directly, perhaps, from eating infected meat, somewhere in south-east Cameroon. It was from this region that researchers began to trace its route.

They sequenced the viruses contained in hundreds of blood samples taken across this vast region of Africa over the course of the twentieth century and preserved in a laboratory in New Mexico. In doing so, they were able to track both the genetic evolution of HIV and its geographical movements. In the 1920s, the first infected person travelled from Cameroon to Kinshasa in the Belgian Congo. From here, the disease gradually spread to neighbouring cities such as Brazzaville, Bwamanda and Kisangani, helped on by increasing urbanization, the boom in transportation and colonial vaccination campaigns. The presence of Haitian workers in this part of Africa during the 1960s probably explains how the virus crossed the Atlantic, and helps to explain why Haitians were overrepresented in the first cases observed in the early 1980s.

By the time this colossal study is published, AIDS has claimed more than 36 million victims worldwide.

# LIGHT

In order to find something of my uncle, you have to follow the road that runs by the river and head upstream. When I asked my mother if there were any of Désiré's friends left in the area, she told me that they had all died long ago. All but one. I found her name in the phone book. One winter's evening, I decided to call her number.

In an old farmhouse in the hills, her ancient telephone rings and, through the receiver, she hears a name she hasn't heard for more than thirty years. After a long sigh, she unspools her memories.

'Ah, Dési, poor kid, though I s'pose we were all kids back then . . . I'm sorry if I can't seem to find the words, but just talking about this makes me all emotional. I wasn't expecting it. The first thing I want you to know is that we had a wild time. You can't imagine how funny Dési was. He was a good friend. We were so bored in the village that all we could think about was finding dumb shit to do. Our parents, they wanted us to do what they did, settle down, get a job. But we didn't give a fuck. We wanted to experience something different. Back then, we were all so left-wing we were practically Maoists. We'd discovered all these ideas at school and university. We wanted to live like the writers we were reading, the musicians we were listening to. Back in the day, pretty much everyone did drugs. We'd missed out on the 1968 student riots and all that stuff, so the least we wanted was to experience drugs. One night, when he was even more bored than usual, Dési just took off for Amsterdam like he was popping down to Nice for a party. We even went to visit him there for a couple of days, but he stayed long after we went back – until your grandmother sent your father to haul him back by the scruff of the neck.

'We tried everything together, spliffs, acid, then smack... It was like an epiphany. I know that's not easy to hear, but once you've tried it, you're blissed, no one can piss you off, and you never want to stop.

'When we got back to the village, we kept using. We'd go buy gear in a couple of bars we knew in Nice, then trawl through the hospital bins to find needles. Sometimes we'd ask the working girls on the Promenade des Anglais to sell us a little dope before heading back to the village, and if they were nice, they'd let us use their works. It was all we thought about. It became our whole life.

'We weren't afraid of an OD. If anything, we'd rather die doing smack than end up living the lives of our parents, working themselves to death. I can't give you the exact date, but I still remember the night we first shot up. We'd just heard on the radio that Pierre Goldman had been murdered. It was a real downer. There we were hoping that the glory days of 1968 would make a comeback, then we realized that people had moved on, that there was no point hoping any more.

'Then, later, the disease showed. At first, we didn't want to believe it. Our families, they were completely fucked up. Your grandparents were like my parents. They'd broken their backs all their lives so their kids didn't want for anything, then suddenly they were in way over their heads. They took it all in their stride. Can't have been easy for them, any more than it was for your father. They had to look after Désiré, Brigitte and then their little girl, poor thing, she'd never done anything to deserve that. Everyone did everything they could, but by then it was too late . . .'

It's the first time I've ever heard someone talk about my uncle like that, with no beating around the bush, no anger. I realize that all that's left of him exists only in the memory of a woman who survived. Before I hang up, somewhat dazed, as though I have been on a journey through time, I thank her for putting into words a life I no longer believed I could bring back into the light.

A NOTE ABOUT THE AUTHOR

Anthony Passeron was born in Nice, France, in 1983. He teaches French literature and the humanities in a secondary school. Published in sixteen languages, *Sleeping Children* is his first novel. It was awarded many prizes in France, including the Prix Wepler and the Prix Première Plume.

A NOTE ABOUT THE TRANSLATOR

Frank Wynne has translated the work of numerous French and Hispanic authors, including Michel Houellebecq, Patrick Modiano, Javier Cercas, and Virginie Despentes. His work has earned him many prizes, including the Scott Moncrieff Prize, the Premio Valle Inclán, and the International IMPAC Dublin Literary Award with Houellebecq for *The Elementary Particles*. His translation of Jean Baptiste Del Amo's *Animalia* won the 2020 Republic of Consciousness Prize.